LARRY ANGELES

AN ADAPTATION OF SHAWN MICHAEL SULLIVAN

NEON BURRITO PUBLISHING

♚ 4 ♛

Cover design by Christina Gubala (xx)

As later discussed, people and places mentioned in this book are being created by the author's words

ISBN: 0692652256
ISBN-13: 9780692652251

I tried to see how I could run off into my own words.

Diane Williams

◉◉◉◉◉◉◉◉

As Larry walks, a memory of his previous day's social blunder wiggles in his
brain.

This mistake had burrowed itself inside his thoughts when he realized after it happened that it had. Its repercussion had been he alone last night, pondering the enormity of his fallibility.

The incident felt to him symbolic of his total imperfection.

Certainly he'd felt hella disappointed and frustrated with himself. He still does, but now he's used to it.

Fixing his mistakes by thinking them into familiarity, then overthinking until he can't take them no more, he shakes this memory off his leg onto the sidewalk where he steps on it as he moves across Hayworth Avenue now.

In the cloudless blue sky above Los Angeles, California, the sun "hangs with itself and rudely stares directly at everyone," to quote a thought Larry might have.

The sun chases him over sidewalks he says, but the sun doesn't even think about Larry, who's partially formed by his external realities, primarily shaped by his *moods*, he's vaguely nonsense, and he American dreams for things to become better as time goes on.

This mood spontaneously bursts in him: "Most people propose to their dreams, it's the rare few who marry." His moods can pop. His daily moods are his pop standards. His moods relate to what time it is, what he's doing, what he might do, and what he does or doesn't notice. His moods calibrate his perspective, bind his rationality. Whenever in a clear mood Larry views the overall world, him a tiny speck within it, then he notices the imperfection of his viewing angle. He recalibrates. He lives, he notices "something else," he recalibrates.

Larry, like most people, would like to feel calibrated to his planet.

It's not happening.

Now His Big Moods, They're Ridiculous.

Ambling across the sidewalk, Larry smiles under Fairfax Cinemas and its closed marquee, this island of shadow outside a boarded-up façade.

It's twelve and a quarter p.m. About his day Larry already wonders what the fuck.

Now headed to the corner of Beverly Boulevard and Fairfax Avenue, also he forgot to install sunglasses before his walk, he squints, a bus hisses to a stop and its doors burst open, then from a walking signal his final seconds tick away.

His thoughts begin to brood while he waits through the next light.

He feels tired these days of worrying about things he needn't worry about, though still these tired days he worries.

He worries about himself if he lets himself. He worries about everything when he does. When he thinks about his worries he feels worried. His worries make his life feel smaller than it can be.

Feeling down but sure he can feel better, while Larry crosses the street he remembers the energy of a non sequitur, which receives freedom from the burden of rationality, and he pictures a quokka.

Feeling better he continues walking.

This then is Larry's walk and his life, neither from one point nor one mood to the next, but a scattering of points mixed with moods.

◉◉◉◉◉◉◉◉

Larry considers the intersection of Hayworth and W 1st adorable.

He figured that out on his own.

Alone and ponderous, he walks with eery silence through other people's quiet neighborhood.

Then he stops walking to stare at the ground for a long moment, not looking at the world (he looks inside himself). Then he hears what sounds like antics. Then he turns to see in a front lawn a toddler playing in a jungle-themed inflatable kiddie pool, a parent watching from a nearby blanket. "Parent and child living the dream," he thinks.

His eyes perform parkour across this street over trees and houses, people and cars, as he thinks, "I desire a life that is not mine but better."

✿❀✿❀✿❀✿❀✿

His backup plan is to tickle his tears until they laugh.

◉◉◉◉◉◉◉◉

Larry spiders across sidewalks as racks webbed with memories and dreams in his mind's wine cellar.

He now and then shakes his feelings at the sun.

He zigzags side-streets to reach his side-thoughts.

Then, after approximately forty-nine minutes, and owing to sweat, thirst, and a misadventure with an insect, he returns to his apartment.

Standing in his living room drinking water by a window and a small black plastic fan, he also texts a friend of his the question of whether the old friend would like to hang, not always savvy about when they two will chill.

It's a scientific fact that Larry wishes now, as he often does, to chill. He wishes to chat outside himself with another person, a friend, and he has three friends. He paces from the living room to his bedroom down the hall and back, also into the kitchen and the bathroom, these being all the rooms in his apartment except his roommate's bedroom.

Pacing his apartment, his emotions feel trapped. He wishes for his walls to crumble. He wishes for his ceiling to pop off. He wishes for his floor and the floor beneath him to vanish and he'll float trapped in the air alone without fear.

Larry has known his old friend since Ohio in their youth, where and when stars peered at their cars with headlights chasing country roads, their favorite music playing on a stereo while they thought, "we can through our lives feel as we feel now, easy, so easy and possible to find rewards in this world we're open to and is open to us," within the classic mold of youth: thinking wishes come into lives as music into ears, which has not been the case for neither Larry nor his friend. But. In their heart their speakers play, music continuing, sometimes quieter, but continuing to play, following the American tradition of being yourself the best you can until you die.

◉◉◉◉◉◉◉◉◉

Not able to tolerate himself alone any longer, Larry now springs(!) himself out of his apartment to hit the sidewalk again, ever the flâneur from life necessity, walking as his mode of transportation for practical and philosophical purposes.

"At least there aren't ceilings above the sidewalks," Larry feels.

He steps outside, the sun's hot breath on his face, though this time he wears sunglasses.

✿❀✿❀✿❀✿❀✿

The misadventure between an insect and Larry on the sidewalk is an important tangential story that exposes aspects of his personality.

Today a scorcher, Larry when he felt something on his neck he presupposed a sweat glob, wondering how "maybe some leaf or other vegetation" had become stuck to him.

He rubbed his neck, there was nothing.

It was a cogitation without incident.

Then he felt something there again, and this time he felt the body of a

8

dime-sized bug.

He then FREAKED out,

wildly,

he swung his body in a fright, rubbing his neck then back, he rubbed his belly, he rubbed the tops of his shoes, shivering with terror in broad daylight on a Los Angeles sidewalk.

For about forty-five seconds he responded like a lunatic to the insect on his neck, then he calmly walked on for ten or so seconds, then he thought about the insect and responded again like a lunatic, for roughly fifteen seconds, and for your information he never pulled the insect off his body nor saw it at all.

There are several stories from Larry's life involving him losing his shit over a bug. Facts verify he has a fear of insects on his body as he has a fear of heights. Fears that don't give him thrills. Fears that remind his emotions of a person's potential to die from random dangers. Fears that do nothing to him but remind his emotions of danger.

And these aren't "dangers" by necessity of their existence, but rather by necessity of describing some fears of his he feels incapable of escaping.

◉◉◉◉◉◉◉◉◉

Larry takes one step down Hayworth, while in his thoughts he takes two steps back, three skips forward, a cartwheel, twelve jumping-jacks, then another step then some other things not being mentioned, in reality passing a middle-age man with gray hair and glasses who each day leans against a beige sedan parked in front of Larry's apartment building.

The gray-haired man stares across the street where a 1940s two-story eight-unit building, one like Larry's, stood across the street until it was recently demolished.

The gray-haired man monitors ongoing construction. Ground has been sunk, a concrete foundation is being assembled for a condominium. Six male construction workers, returning from short breaks they spent sitting on the curb or lawn, they notice Larry as he passes. He notices them. A smile exchange occurs with a young guy who looks like he gives a fuck and he's at his construction job regardless. The guys gear up, put their orange vests back on.

Larry considers his own apartment building's future: his building will be destroyed, its land will be transformed.

His building will vanish from existence except within the sometimes-fragile memories of a few people, whose own existences become sometimes-fragile memories to a few people, and this memory persists at best as a record but never as vibrance, that happens, and what can happen too is those who know the detail of a building's past existence might die without having in their own lives those who might remember them, and records if even kept might not be considered, resulting in immediate vanishment from having existed, that happens too.

Larry relates to buildings with dark fortunes of disintegration, most of all after they've disappeared, been replaced, and must be thought of to exist again.

"If buildings became conscious of cruelty, bliss and chance... if my building had to confront the fact of its mortality..."

Larry feels satisfied with it being true that his building won't learn the facts of mortality, and from buildings he learns one can exist without this lesson.

Then his thoughts about buildings actuate a mood poem: "A burning building roars through its dying, a crumbling building cries from its transience; potential catastrophes from the San Andreas Fault cause buildings to quiver with mortal insecurities."

◉◉◉◉◉◉◉◉

Larry takes steps, recalls something, gets slapped by the sun, wonders something, then he takes a step and enters the gas station where it's his habit to shop.

He notices: a piece of cardboard covers a mysterious disaster on the ground near the electric-door entrance. There's a strong odor of cleaning supply.

The coolers face the racks which face the line of people. This room is the size of a fish bowl. Small such that the line triggers the electric entrance's motion detector. The door whooshes as it opens, then closes then whooshes as long as the line is long.

Beyond glass Maritza behind the register chats with Luciana who sits in the back office. Larry stands behind a line of four people, in his hand a 16oz can with 240mg of caffeine plus other chemicals. He calms his emotions during this time-wasting line (he'd rather be walking around alone!) by glimpsing at the wall above the cooler. He cherishes these slow blinking neon-bordered decorative creatures:

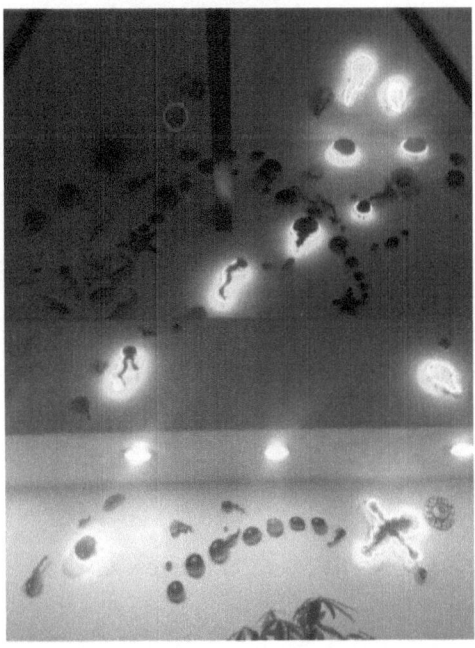

While his eyes scan the wall he hears Spanish from the line's front. Next he hears a British accent. He wiggles his toes in his shoes. He steps forward then he watches a teenage Angeleno hand folded dollar bills to Maritza while carrying a skateboard and a lime cucumber Gatorade Thirst Quencher.

Then an elderly Jewish lady requests lottery tickets while appearing confused about how to use her purse.

Larry stays quiet, familiar with how lines happen. Maritza in her black-rimmed glasses glances at him, smiles. He smiles back.

Then a denim-clad middle-age man speaks Spanish while brown-bagging his tallboy and leaving, Maritza turns to Luciana and says something, and Larry arrives at the cashier window. Maritza turns to him, clicks on her speaker and asks, "Hey! How are you?"

"Good, good," Larry replies while he scans a barcode, the door whooshes, then he asks her in a tone filled with his best wishes: "You?!"

"Oh, the same. The weather, you know," she says while smiling.

He knows for sure. He swipes his debit card. He says, "There's too much weather these days." They exchange elegant nods, she clicks buttons to process their transaction, then she clicks off her speaker and turns back to Luciana.

The odor of cleaning supply clouds this fishbowl. Six people are behind him including, he notices, two blonde Scandinavian men with clean haircuts and black sneakers. He plucks his can from the counter, smiles to Luciana who sees him in her periphery and turns to smile back, then to the back of Maritza's head he waves, aware she can't see him but wanting to send her positive vibes while he steps through the already-whooshed doorway and into the realm of an outside reality dictated by coastal sunshine.

◉◉◉◉◉◉◉◉

Back under the sun again he's mad at it again.

His sidewalk mood shifts into further considering whether the sun, which gives Earth life and humans Vitamin D, if it mistreats him or not. Buildings, alleys are without shadows. He glances at his pathetic foot-long shadow. He sighs. He should be wearing sunscreen, for comfortable body temperature he should be wearing shorts instead of slacks, he should be wearing a hat but he doesn't wear hats, and he concludes the sun mistreats him.

He's frustrated by the potential of his flesh to burn, then peel. Sunlight can cause his skin to freckle, wrinkle, leather. Skin cancer could happen to his gray-eyed body, his moles are potential traitors. This year a sunburn spawned a temporary flesh problem on his forehead, which condition caused him to weigh the sun on a scale of personal safety. He's made plans to visit a general practitioner for discussion. He desires to avoid a day of learning from experience the harshest consequences of overexposure to sunlight, but he has currently failed to expand his efforts to meet this particular desire.

Larry never stops himself from walking through what damages him, sometimes even during the sun's peak afternoon period, often without taking steps toward proper and possible precaution. As today, he fears ultraviolet rays and desires sunscreen after having been under the sun for long enough that he should have already thought of this.

His worries inspire him to think ahead only when he remembers to.

Living in the now, Larry's choice form of living, can turn his perspective myopic and be disadvantageous to his problems, in terms of science. He has to think both now and twenty-minutes-from-now, which sometimes he does, and he can be sorta semi-careful about his daily sunshine intake sometimes.

Though, he's intimidated by his life statistics, which indicate he learns only by his mistakes. He knows his character flaws by pure consequence. He desires for his lessons from mistakes to grow him into a person who doesn't make mistakes, but all that's proven itself to be is desire.

This means he both battles a world that brings him down and battles himself and brings himself down.

He hasn't figured out how to win his battle against himself, which victory he figures would make him king to a land of peaceful moods.

Knowing he should protect himself better, from the sun and bad moods, sweat around his collar, he passes Hayworth Terrace assisted living, sweat on his forehead, the Silverado memory care community across the street.

⊚⊚⊚⊚⊚⊚⊚⊚

Larry now walks to check on his car he parked on Clinton Street following Monday street sweeping.

Ignoring weekly street sweeping results in a ticket. Accordingly, he parks and reparks and parks his car in his neighborhood. It's solely this matter that pressures him toward driving these days.

At Clinton on his car he sees a flyer tucked in a windshield wiper.

He seizes the flyer, reads the pale-green construction paper with its giant font:

We'll Buy Your Car!!!

In Larry's opinion this flyer has aggressive positivity.

He stares at his car's dirty windshield and ill-conditioned body.

"No big deal, doesn't bother me," his emotions decide in a lie to himself, he not thinking much about this yet.

❖❖❖❖❖❖❖❖

Larry is dissimilar to Los Angeles in many ways, though he searches for their similarities.

This city's weather is warmer than his moods on many days. Definitely.

Unlike Los Angeles, Larry's moods experience mild to severe stormy weather on regular occasions.

Sometimes tropical moods bring emergencies, more violence than beauty.

Emotionally speaking, he envies the weather of Los Angeles. His hope is to one day swallow its sun, for his moods to reach seventy-two forever, skin cancer won't exist, and he'll eat all the city lights too, chew the neon to make his blood glow.

These being components toward establishing inside himself the city of Larry Angeles. His urban planning for Larry Angeles being impressive diamond arrangements toward realistic and practical living experiences for a population of people destined for sweet lives of bliss.

◉◉◉◉◉◉◉◉

Larry perceives within himself small and curable levels of embarrassment related to the flyer he removed from the windshield wiper of his dirty seventeen year-old cherry-red car.

His car with its hood paint scrambled, spidering paint cracks on its roof, a rear bumper with blobs of peeled paint, an aged and damaged body from ultraviolet days parked on the street, historical driving misadventures, a 146484 mile odometer, a replaced transmission, stuffing pouring from the torn leather of the driver's seat, and this recent problem the car has had of clicking off, dying, his car stalling, then Larry stays calm and restarts it, his car having not yet died without restarting: though he worries it might die-die on an approaching day, he has no idea why the stalling problem happens to this car which was once his mother's.

With these thoughts bundled inside his emotions he walks around his car.

He then notices on his driver's window, slipped inside black rubber edging, a white business card he snatches and reads: Sell Your Junk Car.

Then he firmly thinks: "Oh that's... something, alright."

He crumbles the snotty business card in his hand with the crummy flyer.

Then he kicks with fury an imaginary object in front of him.

He had much fury and sometimes it's better to be imaginary.

The sun observes him. Larry crosses his arms with two clenched fists and he wonders why he can't stare at the sun and love it, and why can't it love him, why should it burn him and why does he often walk with open vulnerability.

The sun smacks him, smacks the cars, city, everything. The sun is a jerk he feels. He shakes his head. He wonders why him. He wonders how many people had noticed the flyer and card, both of which might've been there since Monday, and what people thought and felt when they noticed. "Did they think down on me and/or my car, and were they entitled to?"

Larry tends to have anxiety about his problems, especially ones that have been noticed by others, and he wonders which ones he has and which ones have been noticed. And who cares and why they care, and who notices but doesn't care through caring or not caring about Larry.

"I don't care about this flyer and card," his emotions plead to him, again lying and wishing they could think and believe what they said.

But the advertisements stimulate Larry's personal perspective on exactly how lousy his life situation is. As his feelings rise again, his angry eyes lift toward the sun, and he says to it with squints, "Today you're up there like an asshole, no clouds want to be around you," his demeanor emboldened by a sunshield he forms with an open palm.

The concept of Larry Angeles is some intra-urban planning bullshit Larry has peddled to the universe each year of his life since his youth and continues to, without he having ever established this miraculous interior city of Larry Angeles.

He has more like a busted up rural town inside his soul.

◉◉◉◉◉◉◉◉

From experience Larry knows: he has to walk this mood off.

Shake it down, walk it off, Larry, the writer says to him.

"Shut up, shut up," Larry thinks to himself as he walks south down Hayworth.

He considers his car situation from an objective perspective, for the purpose of emotional recovery.

"My car is ripe to be sold."

In addition, his moods, through a delusion of reference, wonder if the cosmos spoke to him and he should speak back out of courtesy.

"Plenty of solid reasons why I should sell this dingbat," he tells himself and the universe.

Then as he walks within the city and within himself his emotions recommend to the sun: "Hear me out... when you rise tomorrow stop dead, and hold yourself still for the standard length of a day, then jumpcut to setting, allow the complete night cycle, kiss us with the moon as you do, then rise, repeat, repeat, repeat your normal routine, but include the proposed method of pausing your long day's travel, to truncate the feeling some have of days lasting forever... a day's length determined by the Earth's rotation, this planet is spherical, plus there are plants and also I'm emotional, I'll get scientists to work on hatching this scheme or, no, to make an impossible plan exist I'll pretend for a moment that science doesn't exist, and science can't stop me because science doesn't control my imagination. Although reality is indeed science, so science is fact, this means my thoughts have their own science."

"Sun, back to the plan, you'd be both arriving and leaving when you'd be around... and you'd create the large shadows where I long to stand."

"You'd look wonderful, so cool, with slick moves. I promise."

A portion of the thoughts Larry then broadcasts into the universe, with hopes of the sun hearing him: "Style has science but isn't science... since pure style exists outside facts..."

✿❀✿❀✿❀✿❀✿

In reality, Larry Angeles is an unincorporated community in Greene County, Ohio.

It's located between Bellbrook and Xenia on Interstate 35. It has a crow for a sheriff and an alligator as a postmaster. Its population consists of four witches and a warlock who live in a big, old Quercus alba (white oak).

Humans once lived in Larry Angeles but no one remembers who or why, unfortunately. The town has six empty buildings including the post office, police station, a library and a historical museum. A lobster once laid foundation for the construction of a public television station that was never completed, owing to the lobster experiencing private disasters including losing his husband to death, the lobster then moving to live alone on the volcanic island of Therasia, Greece.

Being a community founded on principles of self-sufficiency, the rural town of Larry Angeles doesn't include the mainstream option of a single convenience store.

Fuck That is the official town motto, referring to anything/everything told by someone to someone else about how that person should choose to live.

⊙⊙⊙⊙⊙⊙⊙⊙⊙

Again crossing Beverly, Larry thinks, "Thanks for listening to me earlier, sun. That was my ooh-la-oops. For some outlandish reason I was having a mood that felt like an idea. Asking you to pause and... you know, I'm embarrassed I had that idea and shared it with you."

Larry's body behavior shifts into telling the sun, "Sorry, I'm upset about something else. I want only to love you. Thanks for solar power."

He supposes there's something to think about besides the sun pissing him off, the crummy flyer and the business card.

He thinks to himself, "I'm acting like hullabaloo... I'm being a bunch of static yacking and that's not all I am."

"These are only my feelings, under the blue skies near the Pacific Ocean. This whole bit about about my sun anxiety could be removed from my life's story if I wore sunscreen, a hat, and/or carried a sun umbrella."

"If only I were what's called proper!"

Then Larry's emotions tell his thoughts, "Selling my car to not have it sounds better than having it, since I don't care about my car at all. And it doesn't help this nice neighborhood look any better…"

✿❀✿❀✿❀✿❀✿

Using a metal detector, Larry searches the beach of his moods for lost pirate's booty.

"Where's the pirate's booty?" he wonders.

"Today could be the day I find it," he thinks as he makes circles on the sand with his metal detector, his lips on the straw of a virgin margarita.

He dawdles the blocks and dawdles his thoughts.

Phenomenology his life, Larry's senses his self, he looks at fronds in a palm tree and there he is. A light wind brushes his slacks against his legs, same as carss across Beverly, buildings and streets smell like armpits, in addition to whatever else exists with him he absorbs it as he dilly-dallies.

This city in him, him wondering how he's in this city.

Then his thoughts slow to a lollygag and he feels fine. Then he pictures an alligator walking like a human. Then he spaces out under the sun.

◉◎◉◎◉◎◉◎◉

The healthiest and calmest mood is no mood, and a fantastic and famous location for practicing this philosophy is Southern California.

There are those in SoCal who live outside madness. Totally. Life beyond contrived cynicism. And their salvation isn't from the arts alone, but through for example the ocean, yoga, and/or meditation. How can a person say worry is better than meditation? Here the ocean reminds people of waves in their lives, and Larry can read more to become more worried, but one doesn't go to the beach to find a worry.

Below Beverly Larry stares through the front window of Psychic Boutique, at its neon sign, its yellow leather couch, its circular glass table. The room is vacant but its neon lit. This room is like him. He appreciates the tradition and need for psychics. He knows there are real and phantom problems in his life, and another person can help him spot the difference.

"I want to know who I'll become, since I can't guess, and I seem to be isolating myself from reality."

Then a thing he'd call a fact does what he'd call hits him: "It's irresponsible and risky to consider selling my car without being able to replace it."

Larry's feelings think he's on to something. "I don't know my future or what may come of it, and friends visit and events occur and things like that, and adults need cars for certain standard life circumstances, including I might need a car for a future job situation, so I should have a car. However awful my car is what I can say about my car is it's mine."

"My car reminds me of me and I'm going to keep it. Thanks though, outrageous ads from the cosmos," his thoughts say, employing sarcasm.

His metal detector scans the beach.

"Where's the pirate's booty?"

"I should wash my car soon," he thinks while he remembers bird poop on his car too.

He pretends to adjust the rim of his hat when he's not wearing a hat. He doesn't make this motion, he doesn't move his hand, because he doesn't have to move his hand to pretend.

◎◎◎◎◎◎◎◎

This narrative of Larry would be different if his life were different, as it has been different before, with different places and people, but this being his current life this is his current narrative and that's the way things are.

"If only my life was different from how it is... If only it were better!" Every day these days Larry thinks this multiple times for a plethora of reasons.

Feelings from his life have taken place in *The Great Gatsby*, now he feels more that he's in "The Crack-Up".

He does about things what he can, living on the street where Fitzgerald died.

What he does now is he leaves his apartment again, having circled back to drink water and use the bathroom, now he walks one-block south from Hayworth to Oakwood Avenue, to walk west to La Cienaga Boulevard.

He listens to Joy Division on his headphones and continues to dance within his glass-cage of moods as a stripper for emotions, having forgotten to re-install sunglasses.

✿❀✿❀✿❀✿❀✿

An example of a story from this same city, different year, different Larry:

the moonroof open, chill music from the stereo, a girl recently moved from Portland in his car's passenger seat, he drives her and his camera friend across Mulholland Drive through the hills, Los Angeles on their left, the Valley to their right, the three of them headed toward Mulholland Dam, without a goddamn worry in anyone's mind, on this January 2012 night their feelings are but the bliss of being with others for an evening excursion, their adventure is on their mind, pure, and this adventure goes well, the camera friend brought six bottle rockets they fired off while listening to Madonna's *Confessions on a Dance Floor* from a phone, taking sips from beers they'd brought, enjoying the crisp and cool California nighttime.

Larry would like the writer to release this statement:

"The Larry Angeles urban plans include details related to shade being present throughout the city above sidewalks, from spectacular shade trees, and clever cityscape designs, including some areas resembling glass neon tunnels, and some areas feeling as if blankets dangle overhead but actually it's air-landscape."

"Though in the very center of the city there'll be one large garden with relaxed admission rates, Sun Garden. This place will also feature impressive artistic ornamentations, and friendly animal codes. including ones related to habitated buffalo and zebra... and this is for there to be a place in Larry Angeles where full-time lovers of the sun can soak it up."

"Since the city of Larry Angeles will have a massive population that's brilliantly assembled, this Sun Garden will be enormous and have a lake at its center, this'll have a vegetarian Loch Ness monster, there'll be a vegan Bigfoot, in a forest section, and most of the park will be open field for garden work and joie de vivre."

"Anywhere/everywhere in the city, in addition to train tracks, and paths for bikes and rollerskates and skateboards and hoverboards, all roads lead to its center, Sun Garden. There will be a parking lot in a thick ring around this place which is the size of a baker's dozen theme parks, and people will head to it for buying from stores in their hearts and going on rides in their souls."

"I hope visitors use sunscreen but, that's up to each of them. Also, there's the possibility of teleportation being existent for travel... presently undecided."

"Yet I don't imagine myself ever, ever daytripping to this wonderful Sun Garden."

"Though I see it clearly as the center to the gem city in my dreams. A symbol of the force and faculty of nature... nature, which is more important than words for example, the word tulip less important than a living tulip, the word bush less important than a living bush, and the word sun less important than the living sun."

"Here, then, is a prolepsis: mellifluous — a word that illustrates and describes the potential mood-altering impact of words. What I think this illustrates is people's potential to craft their lives into words."

"But, overall, to keep writing one keeps living. During any moment a person is alive, it's really life that's most happening."

"Point is, people like me will go to Sun Garden near dark, and there's going to be a nighttime variation named Neon Garden..."

He walks north on La Cienaga to walk east on Clinton to walk south on Fairfax. From there he walks to Oakwood to walk to Beverly to link back to La Cienaga to walk around some more.

Across these streets Larry most frequently engages in flânerie, in order to give himself the illusion of being less alone in this world, in reality taking long trips to nowhere with no one and for no reason.

Summary of the recent: a portion of existence is compacted on this hot mess planet voyaging time, and Los Angeles is a microcosm for some of the main forms by which humans battle to endure with bitter glory their struggle through the reality of universal chaos.

Plus: each street in this city's grid reminds Larry of himself, his emotions a grid of streets in his brain.

Larry searches for what one might call mystical solutions to his life's problems.

He searches for discovery, he searches for harmony, he searches for marvelous happenstances to swing his way.

One too might call his quest bullshit.

Larry hopes to remain calm when he can.

He hopes to maybe encounter a person who wants to be on the City Council of Larry Angeles. He hopes to bump into such people, whom he will know because, "we'll share dynamic conversations about sideshows, *Rebels of the Neon God*, life as a package of feelings, art as a moment captured in crystal, similar to the *Jurassic Park* DNA principle..."

"Or if a person isn't familiar with my favorite topics, may it be that we find a way to be mellow with each other."

"My preference is for non-violent creatives whose main hobbies are snacks and animals."

"When I don't feel my strongest, my moods depend on another person's."

Larry supposes City Council members for Larry Angeles could be anywhere in Los Angeles. "Could be anyone! And if we met," this he feels he knows so he thinks is true, "we'd battle together this world for our own. But we might never meet..."

His whole life Larry has remembered, when he has, that he lives in a mammoth eight-billion people global circumstance. "In addition, there are shared achievements from humans spanning time, including being conscious of time and other figuring outs, and this my life is in the future that was once imagined... a new future can be imagined from today."

"A future when the universe has a map, and space travel is cake. I live in the stone age of technology. But I enjoy my own days, with their modicum of mystery..."

He thinks now about these things and similar important matters related to the engineering of Larry Angeles as he walks west across Beverly, until another thought enters his mind through his stomach.

◉◉◉◉◉◉◉◉

After minutes have spun their digital hands, the sun has rotated position, "thank God," Larry has rotated his moods and he walks into Benito's to order a burrito.

He pays for his burrito on his debit card. His sales receipt doesn't have a tipping option. He never carries cash, at other places he leaves friendly tips from his debit card, when there's the option but, again, here this isn't, so he can never leave money in the styrofoam **T I P S** cup. This being a place he visits on regular occasion he always wonders what he should do about his guilt related to tip money. On occasion he daydreams of leaving a one-hundred dollar bill, of that being easy for him to do.

Resorting to what is easy for him now he does nothing, he returns his debit card to his wallet, then he leaves his typical eatery, which neighbors his typical gas station.

He enters the gas station.

"Heeeey baby, how are you?" Luciana asks him as he enters.

He smiles because she smiles. "Made it through yesterday, hell yeah, how are you?!"

"Fiiiiine," she says, she smiles, he smiles, "thank you," they exchange elegant nods, she looks at the shelves she's stocking, he looks at sour gummy worms. The age of his mother, Larry considers Luciana part of the backbone of Los Angeles. He appreciates her as he does his mother.

He considers buying sour gummy worms, this interest up against fruit and yogurt snacks.

He might anyway decide on a blueberry danish and chocolate milk.

Or perhaps a chocolate bar, maybe something with coconut, conceivably peanut butter, and then out the door he walks waving and smiling to Maritza at the register, she smiling back, he holding a Mexican snack cake that comes in a plastic wrapper which unwrapped has two chocolate cakes each partitioned in individual wrappers, and he bought strawberry milk.

He returns to Benito's. Enrique slides across the counter a tray with a California burrito. Larry says, "Thanks." Enrique normal nods. Larry considers Enrique's peppered goatee fabulous upon his deep-lined face, he sits down, he reads Bukowski's *Factotum* on his phone as he eats his burrito.

Thinking about it now, he doesn't understand why he chose strawberry milk. He opens the strawberry milk, takes a sip, bites into his burrito, chews and reads.

While reading his ebook his good old friend texts him back: *chillin*.

Larry smiles, finishes reading a paragraph, takes a bite of his burrito, texts back: *headed*, this their usual plan-making procedure.

Then Larry pauses and sits quietly on his stool by the window, taking a mental nap. He stares out the window at the gas station sidewalk on Beverly and Fairfax. A homeless man he regularly encounters in his neighborhood, a youngish man who will say to Larry, "I like *Back to the Future*, do you have a dollar," he stands by the street with his face pointed toward the ground, glancing up at cars when they stop at a red light. Larry watches him notice a person roll down their car window as he walks toward their car, the passenger hands him two dollar bills, and he thanks the passenger whose car drives away from the green light, hen he walks back to stand at the sidewalk until the next red light.

The man doesn't walk toward a car. He stares at the ground through the next red light.

Larry hears conversation between Benito's employees in the kitchen while Adán "Chalino" Sánchez plays from speakers.

He reads a page and a half while eating his burrito, then he walks as the sun dips into the sky's other side, larger and longer shadows coming now from trees and buildings.

He welcomes the approaching night and walks in shadows. He heads to his old friend's place, walking across Beverly reading *Factotum* and unwrapping his snack cakes.

This old friend has known Larry for over fifteen years, having gone to a Seventh-day Adventist K-12 school with him.

They were aware of each other before they were friends, but friends from when this old friend was a junior in high school.

"After school one day, back when we were taking… um... TCM: Transition to College Math together, he drove me home in his busted-up Corsica for some reason and whatever... all the best Ohio friendships were formed over trips across country roads, " to quote a thought this old friend might have.

After the old friend graduated from high school, he lived with Larry in a Kent State dorm room for one semester. Then they left together, returning to their three-hour distant hometowns, outside suburbs outside the city of Dayton, and there they waited until they both moved to California, again living together in Mission Viejo, Orange County eleven years ago.

Through these eleven years they each lived in multiple other locations with multiple other people, leading now to them living seven blocks from each other.

"Sierra Bonita Avenue is easy walking distance," Larry feels, in relation to where his old friend lives.

◉◉◉◉◉◉◉◉

Larry stands outside his friend's apartment and reads his phone. A text from his friend tells him: *can't hang today, sorry.*

"What kind of chillin' is this??" his feelings wonder.

He stomps his foot, an emotional symbol for 'All I wanted was to be around a person, for crying out loud!'

But Larry doesn't often get what he wants.

He stomps his foot again.

Then he realizes there's nothing to be upset about here, his friend had even apologized.

He wishes he had a strategic personality. He wishes he could get a grip on his life, clench this world, but he can't get a grip so he takes out his phone to read lines from *Factotum*.

Then, sarcasm returning to this thoughts, he thinks "Terrrrific!"

Then his feelings begin to sing Hallelujah while he texts to his old friend's roommate, Larry's friend the poet: *let's capitalize this night.*

Larry waits a moment, thinks about it, worries, then he clarify-texts: *let's hang out.*

Larry's friend the poet met him and his good old friend back in Mission Viejo eleven years ago.

They'd been three in a group of thirteen friends sharing trials, misfortunes and perseverances within the tried lines of disgruntled young adults attending community college, believing their lives to be set in a post-apocalyptic allegory, having fits of feelings new to them and drinking their fits away at parties, feeling uninspired by the adult planet, over time finding themselves transitioning into being unimpressive within it.

The poet grew himself blue-collar. It oozes from him, his full beard, his glasses. He straight talks. He taught himself, he listens to blues and jazz, plays the guitar, has tattoos. He lived in multiple places along his road toward living close to Larry, including nine months in Korea Town, Los Angeles alone as an alcoholic, the story which the poet is converting into a prose book.

The poet and Larry both enjoy reading and consider themselves capable as writers.

They've co-written two poetry books: *Frank Zappa & Barry Manilow* and *the name of this book is untitled but that's a bit of a lie.*

⊙⊙⊙⊙⊙⊙⊙⊙

Pacing a small lap on the sidewalk in front of the apartment of his old friend and the poet, Larry to a movie friend of his also texts: *whatchya doin?*

After sending that text and while pacing, he stares at his phone's text screen, wondering why he sent that text, wondering what he expects to happen because of it. He often wonders about texts he sends his movie friend, whom he calls this since they desire to make movies together, this being a text Larry sent him yesterday:

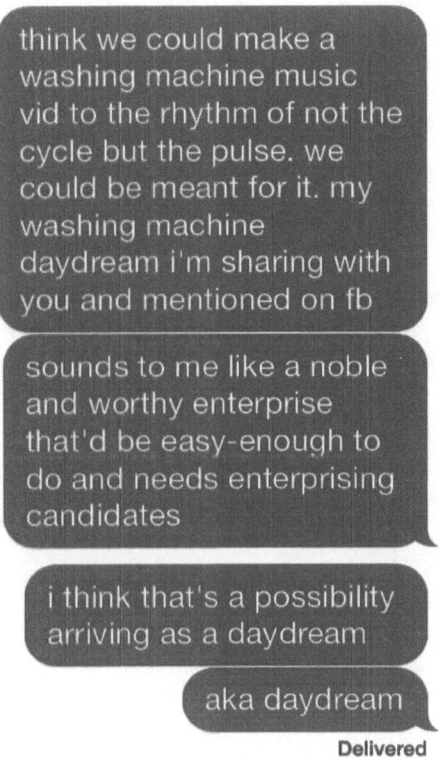

think we could make a washing machine music vid to the rhythm of not the cycle but the pulse. we could be meant for it. my washing machine daydream i'm sharing with you and mentioned on fb

sounds to me like a noble and worthy enterprise that'd be easy-enough to do and needs enterprising candidates

i think that's a possibility arriving as a daydream

aka daydream

Delivered

His movie friend he doesn't see often...

While on the sidewalk draining time, Larry's moods easily spot the many frustrations in his current moment.

His moods now protest through toddler hysterics. They angrily think-yell subconsciously: "This, fucking goddamnit... this is the day off!"

Larry is glad to have this day away from the teenage job he has an adult, which job he's grateful for, he remembers to be grateful for anything that happens in his life at all, but regarding his precious spare time today he wonders, "How can this be how I spend my life's time, and what I do, think and feel, how can this be it?"

He fears his day off work is also his day off life, which fear scares him tons.

"How many days have I taken off from my life?"

"How many of my days have been and might be nonsense..."

Then, thinking big-picture, Larry engages in calming metamorphosis through transitional thoughts: including the accumulated amount of human history so far experienced by everyone, the total conscious time humans have existed on this planet, Larry begins hopeful long-term goal wishing that what's happened won't constitute even half of what will happen to humans, not even a quarter.

He's big-dreams hoping that humans, on this planet, and out elsewhere when necessary, he's hoping as if it's already true that humans are in the early years of their existence and they'll make it into their elder years or learn to live without end.

Perhaps there will be no end to the amount of time humans spend alive in the cosmos.

"Humans are kids."

His friend the poet texts back: *I'm working late tonight.*

"Life is what it is, that's true," Larry thinks.

It's not his worries he wants to think about, so where is the topic outside his worries he wonders.

"As tribute to the nightmarish beauty and magic of Hollywood, the building where the Larry Angeles City Council meetings take place will — not would, as in if, but will, as in definitely — be named Tod Browning."

"It won't be called The Tod Browning Building."

"It will be called Tod Browning."

"And Tod Browning will have two parking lots, connected together by a middle bridge, and the parking lots will be named Daisy and Violet Hilton, in honor of the American dream in a fever."

⊙⊙⊙⊙⊙⊙⊙⊙

While the sun nears sleep on a purple-orange horizon, Larry takes a slow stroll west across Beverly back toward his apartment, this richly colored sunset boosting his mood.

As slow as you want, the writer suggests.

Larry thinks, "The darkness of night is coming, and I adore artificial lights, the city's own shine, and at night when it's quiet, when me and most people are inside living serene lives of quiet beauty, then I am alone listening to Soko, my room's small white plastic fan whirling, the murmuring of the city a sound floating through open windows behind my blue curtains, anyway thanks for beginning to set now, sun, and kisses."

The evening sky is mellow as fuck-yeah and Larry feels better.

Here in Los Angeles he thinks the world is wonderful so he should feel wonderful.

Larry tries to push his reality toward his thought of feeling wonderful, and he implements a helpful observation w/exclamation, "Got the miraculous going on around me!"

Larry feels now, "I'll count every beautiful thing I see along this sidewalk. Beauty is everywhere to be found and I exaggerated about how much counting I'll do. I'm trying to say when I don't look for good in the world that's bad decision making. The search for good is worth it since the bad is easy to find, on the surface."

"And good can be on the surface as well, as this fucking sunset tonight demonstrates, hell yeah."

"My life is partially a matter of what I allow myself to notice."

Having returned to his apartment building, Larry back-alley paces, his worries tucked away from view.

"I don't want to be certain that life is bad. I don't want to be a person who gives examples of the bad. I don't want to be known to say, 'The temperature of this room is cold, life is bad.' I don't want to be known to say, 'I just remembered how dirty my room is, life must be awful, why do I keep doing this to myself and why must I live.'

"I don't want to hear an insult from another person about me and seriously think, 'What even is the point of anything, oh my god, seriously.'

"I don't want to be a person who's on edge. Over the edge is surely the place for me. But there are two edges to fall from and, specifically, may it be that I fall my way over the edge into happiness. Gonna be such a badass happy person, according to my bucket list."

Then Larry begins to walk away from his apartment again, down Fairfax at night.

He thinks of what his friend Ragavan said to him during seventh grade, Our days are long, our years are short.

His moods stir around his current thoughts. "My day depends on my day and me. Me, am I looking for a good day, or am I looking for a bad day. Oh I tend to find what I go looking for."

"Except happiness, actually."

"And, when I sound narcissistic, which is a popular life model these days, well I need others at least equal to how I need myself, and I hope when I sound narcissistic that doesn't mean I live by narcissism, since others make me exist..."

"Also I want to read more about hedonism and amorality, and engage with the feeling of being a human along with eight-billion others living in this future that's becoming the past."

There's a difference between places where Larry's feet might go and places where his thoughts might go.

Duh.

BUT ALSO, the places where Larry's feet go affect his thoughts and dreams.

He's a citizen of Los Angeles wishing, along with others, for this city to make his life feel as big as his imagination becomes when he sees this city.

He wants to feel, for example, as if he is the intersection of La Brea Avenue and Beverly Boulevard.

He thinks that would indeed be something. "Right there on Beverly and La Brea is my everything, and I consider my everything epitomized in different areas through distinct qualities around many parts of Los Angeles, but currently I'm referring to the two gas stations, Lulu cafe, Schwartz Bakery, Domino's Pizza, Starbucks Coffee, Susina Bakery & Cafe, a strip mall with Wok Master and a yogurt place and a videogame store and a cell phone store, a movie theater (owned and operated by Quentin Tarantino), Baba Ghanooj, all right there across the street and next to each other, and I dream and dream again of feeling as big as even that intersection."

Describing physical places where Larry's feet go describes his ideal emotional cityscape, according to presentation materials being assembled toward construction fundraising for Larry Angeles.

So, viewing descriptions of Los Angeles as beneficial toward understanding the ludicrous engineering schemes of Larry Angeles, the writer would like to mention the intersection Larry described is one-and-two-tenths mile distant from where he lives.

On the corner of Fairfax and Beverly one block from his apartment is CBS Television City, where "The Price Is Right" is shot, a television game-show currently hosted by Ohioan Drew Carey. It has a long, golden rep within the American television community. Larry thinks about that show: "Represent."

A block south down Fairfax is an outdoor mall named The Grove. This is the location of a bookstore where Larry works, and where there are a variety of stores people go to these days, common celebrity visitors, an attached multiplex, along with restaurants of varying types.

The outdoor mall on W 3rd Street is adjacent to a consortium of eateries named The Original Farmers Market. Larry eats from here French crêpes served to him by Filipinos with diamond-stud earrings. Or at one of the two American-tradish diners. The longest lines can be for Brazilian BBQ.

The market nests across the street from a Trader Joe's, which nests across the street from a glassy, squat and rotund Writers Guild of America, West building, which nests across the street from a strip mall with CVS/ pharmacy, Whole Foods Market and K-Mart, which nests across the street from The Grove and The Original Farmers Market.

Most of the daily essentials a citizen needs to live Larry can find to purchase in one of the four corners of this Fairfax and W 3rd Street intersection near his apartment and where he works.

◎◎◎◎◎◎◎◎

Sauntering in front of K-Mart now in the evening, Larry prefers when creative perspectives are in his thoughts, compared to when his worries are.

A certain topic of his day is lodged in his mind: "There's a conceptual difference between a fact and a feeling."

"A fact is a piece of reality."

"A feeling is a piece of a personal reality."

"A fact can be a word, a word can compose a feeling, and this can become reality on a piece of paper."

"But reality is cosmic sized to a factual degree that doesn't make it all the way to paper."

"My reality isn't composed of my words, it's composed of more, that's a healthy thing for me to remember."

"Then I realize my thoughts and feelings aren't reality."

The glass K-Mart door opens, he enters into this fabulous realm of fluorescent lights.

"Science describes the facts of reality, I describe the feelings of mine."

Then Larry descends into the K-Mart basement to ramble through consumerism, in the store and in his thoughts, side-longing for a gorgeous biomechanical utopia.

"My reality, my life, feels different than appearances suggest, based on reports I hear back in words from others. Often when I hear people describe me, not a single feeling I experience gets mentioned. Often because the other person didn't think of it. Reality is of course bigger than a perspective on me and my life. Reality is bigger than how another person sees me and how I see myself. Which is helpful since people sometimes, some more than others, it's part of their character, they take pride in always immediately knowing words for the worst. Which is a quality I don't admire any longer, though I did as a teenager."

"As a teenager I grew the belief that an apocalypse happened after each disappointment I experienced. 'This problem is the end of the world,' I'd feel each time, but really I treated myself like royalty," (reminder, Larry can't even become the king of his moods,) "and I related to people who described their lives as such an experience... I'd still think each disappointment in my life was an apocalypse if I hadn't already experienced a life's list of apocalypses."

"I no longer wish to conceive myself as destined to comprehend and experience the apocalypse."

"Glory lies in discovering not problems but their solutions."

"The world needs an anti-apocalypse vibe."

The writer agrees. Like most depressives, Larry can't quite say what's wrong, but he knows something is, and he's beginning to see that part of what's wrong is himself, his occasional gloomy attitude for example. Unless sharing is happening, no one feels better from hearing another person's gloom. A mutual best case scenario is a person feels low and worried but they hear another person's low worries then they both feel terrible. Maybe they can notice who feels more terrible. That might be helpful. It's simply that most people don't have trouble finding gloom. Gloom isn't practical or helpful in the adult planet. The adult planet has other things to think about. That's how the adult planet made itself. By thinking about making itself. Not by thinking about what can bring people down, but what can lift them.

Larry stands in the toy aisle by the board games in the corner with the bikes on racks to the left. Then he pokes around the book section, snakes through the entertainment section, then he takes the escalator back to the first floor and looks through the men clothing department before leaving.

On Fairfax north of Beverly is Melrose Avenue, north of which is Santa Monica Boulevard, then there's a portion of the city-within-a-city West Hollywood, heading north to Sunset Boulevard, north of which is Hollywood Boulevard, where Hollywood is, eastern travels leading one into the nexus, onto the Walk of Fame, past Madame Tussauds, a Scientology Information Center, Ripley's Believe It or Not, Guinness World Records Museum, The El Capitan Theatre, Grauman's Chinese and Egyptian Theatres, etc.

Grauman's Egyptian Theatre is three-and-two-tenths miles from Larry's apartment. Seldom times he traverses this specific path. Larry considers that his walking perimeter's outer limits, since beyond there it sounds to him like *walking*.

Although within a single mile radius of interlocked streets he can meander six to ten miles no problem. He tricks himself and loops his thoughts into repeating, "this walk with this short trip back home," forging foundations for illusions that gift him his longest walks and renew his license as a flâneur.

Melrose is nearest Larry, at an intersection with Fairfax High School. Down this Fairfax spot are locally-famous businesses: the Cinefamily at the Silent Movie Theatre (a 1942 building with a history of movies and murder), Family Bookstore, HUF, The Hundreds, Supreme, The Golden State, and two-handfuls of et cetera.

Larry lives four blocks down from Melrose, a block west of Fairfax. This area being called the Fairfax District. The book *How To Get Into the Twin Palms* is set here. Also, there's an Orthodox Jewish Community, with many Jewish-owned and themed businesses. Larry's favorite clothing stores are Goodwill on Beverly and the Jewish Council Thrift Shop on Fairfax. His apartment building sits directly behind Canter's, a Jewish delicatessen with a solid reputation, classic diner waiters and waitresses who know how to think of others, and the notable Kibitz Room.

The Kibitz Room is a place famous musicians have visited, e.g. Neil Young and Guns N' Roses, for the ability a small bar's stage has to become an island of paradise for music.

Music establishes dreamscapes in the feelings of most if not all people.

That's behind his apartment and, to repeat, Larry wonders how much of the city is in himself and how much of himself is in the city.

There's cultural noise in this area of Los Angeles where Larry lives, Mid-City West.

Places he's visited in circumstances related to him remaining open to the world as it comes to his life in forms he cannot control and so adores, trying not to fear the size of his life each day, accidentally fearing his life during unsteady stretches but, human, accidents happen, point is most of the mentioned places aren't particles from Larry's recent life being assembled into this verbal portrait of him as he is today, but they're being mentioned without narrative intention, continuing here on page as in his life, as glittery aesthetics reminding him to strive as a midnight marauder for bliss from trash culture that mutates people into current personalities with contemporary disillusion, since anything not mentioned in this text doesn't exist in the world as it's being described, and many of the mentioned places are seen by Larry as tokens to phenomenal days from his real and imagined history and future.

The writer considers this a note worth making since after all it's true that a future when Larry is gone has too days when these buildings will vanish, then perhaps become forgotten, then perhaps the word Los Angeles will mean nothing and Hollywood never existed.

◉◉◉◉◉◉◉◉

Back inside his apartment, in his bedroom, he turns on his fan, kicks off his kicks, wonders what the hell is even the point of anything at all.

He feels he must give his sadness the slip and retreat back inside books as always.

He plucks John Fante's *1933 Was a Bad Year* from a stack of books by his bed and tv.

Larry admires Fante's torch as a human made dually by his words and reality.

Larry craves these flames tonight. He begins a patient read. He absorbs sentences to cherish them. The lush literary vibrancy of Fante's intoxicating regionalism, his persistent and outrageous romanticism.

Larry throws his heart at this book, but his heart doesn't stick. He wishes he could love this book like he wants to.

The review his feelings are drafting on page thirty-nine: "This isn't set in Los Angeles as The Bandini Quartet, and it not being set in Los Angeles is a cheap and easy, shallow criticism for me to make, the exact type of badness I'm trying to evict from myself, yes I think so, and this book's problem must be deeper. Honest writing comes from honest relationships between the power of words in text and the power of words in the writer's life, and Fante writing about Los Angeles while living in Los Angeles is his most honest and best writing because he could see his words within the city where they had their meaning."

He glares at *1933 Was a Bad Year* like he's pissed at it, though he isn't though he kind of is, because he wishes it gave him the surge in passions he fancies, though as angry as he gets at the book his problems aren't the book's fault tonight.

Thing is, Larry's moods oscillate regarding words in general.

There are emotional moments when to him all books seem like horseshit fundamentally cruel by nature of words being able to feel more beautiful than his life feels.

If Larry's life felt written... He thinks then he'd treasure his life more. If life could be written, *if my life could be redrafted!* is a thought he's had and has.

"I wish," he wishes, "that from the cloud of words which I call existence, I could find a ship hidden within the cloud waiting to fly me elsewhere."

Fante is a hero to him but, Larry feels, currently, solid on his night's reading having ended, a half page after beginning.

◉◉◉◉◉◉◉◉

Larry shuts off his lights, takes out his laptop, checks his e-mail, Instagram, Twitter and Facebook.

Then he has a quick chat with an Internet friend, whom he knows from a movie site. They are citizens of the Internet who know and live alongside each other.

They chat about how Larry didn't go to the Tao Lin and Mira Gonzalez reading at Skylight Books he'd said he'd be going to, since he didn't have anyone to go with and didn't go alone.

Larry mentions to his friend he's writing a novella he feels he'll finish.

This friend is a book person, familiar and fond with writers that being fond and familiar with makes a person fond and familiar with the nature and possibility of reading and writing. Keywords: fond/familiar, reading/writing.

Larry's Internet friend goes to a university in India that sounds like a big-deal school, he's mentioned studying business.

Going to a fine school for a solid reason is actually one of the well-known plans for a smooth landing on adult planet. "Nice," is what Larry thinks about his friend's life plan.

This friend often expresses to Larry distress over "boilerplate internal dysfunction," sharing which private information results in Larry relating.

Being on the Internet chatting with others is like reading a book as it's being written, in terms of the safe distance between words and reader and the capacity people and words have to surprise an audience.

Larry is familiar with people in certain circumstances repivoting their life's perspective owing to another person. This isn't a strategy he's invented, people like him who experience this will often notice the very same thing: one can feel alone-alone in this world, conjure a world that misunderstands them, underappreciates them, and sees too differently for possible coexistence, then the same person another day can meet a person who agrees, they relate, they instantly each feel less alone, and now they feel their yesterday's-rebellion against the world was absurd, misguided, and their yesterday's belief isn't their worry today.

Not every worry is necessary. Larry's Internet friend says he'll read the novella. Hearing this causes Larry to feel happy because he knows at least someone will read it.

He feels connected to a cosmic chain of people who adore literature. He now and then observes phantom patterns of what he calls internal realism, since all that's fake but gives meaning has equal capacity to what's real and gives meaning, emotionally speaking.

⊙⊙⊙⊙⊙⊙⊙⊙

On his television begins *The Great Escape*.

Larry's been watching this movie for over a week now, in mostly ten minutes increments, while he drifts into sleep.

There've been a few instances of him deliberating rewatching some scenes that upon seeing he thought they needed rewatching.

He's been enjoying this movie he last saw years ago at the Nuart Theatre, during a United Artists 90 years celebration. Larry when he first saw this movie it didn't impress him, years ago he didn't think it was anything but movie make-believe. But he appreciates *The Great Escape* these nights. Its characters feel shaped like people who require bravery from certain disparate perspectives, of spectral importance, and they coalesce as fabulous prisoners of war. He appreciates how the movie forms a logical structure within the imprisoned soldier social network desiring high-number escapes and professional retaliation against a foul enemy.

MASH made prophecy of the emotional prosperity *The Great Escape* has brought Larry, and *From Here to Eternity* will confirm that he enjoys war movies now, which movie genre he wouldn't have expected himself to ever cherish as he currently does.

The backdrop of war to human drama gives emotions a particular focus and characters a rich clarity, which he's come to admire from a narrative perspective.

⊙⊙⊙⊙⊙⊙⊙⊙

Two nights prior, Larry had realized his *The Great Escape* blu-ray, which he'd bought nine weeks ago, during an early Father's Day sale at Best Buy, his blu-ray skips at the 1hr40min portion of the movie.

When the escape is about to happen!

Larry had checked his receipt and found the allowable time for merchandise return was past. He'd examined the blu-ray it appeared normal, its malfunction was invisible. Then he'd explored his viewing possibilities. *The*

Great Escape fully functions at 2hr10min. So tonight he's going to watch from 2hr10min again, having his previous night watched from there until 2hr38min (close to the movie's end).

Larry intends tonight to start back at the beginning of the end portion of the movie available to him, to engage again the final circuit, since he likes this movie and everything.

He feels trained and prepared for this endeavor.

Except Larry isn't watching *The Great Escape* yet. It plays on his tv, riveting dramatic stuff, people either escaping or being killed, Steve McQueen in a famous motorcycle scene, which the movie passes through while Larry feels sexual. Something about his nights at their close can sometimes sweep him into his private sexy feelings, then alone in his room he looks at porn on his computer.

The Great Escape on tv, he watches JOI porn, a concept enchanting his recent curiosities. JOI stands for Jerk Off Instrument, and it's a vision for porn in which women with strong personalities are clad in sexual undergarments and talk smut to the camera. They imagine the man watching, dictating how the man should masturbate. Larry thinks this is healthy, consensual porn. He's being openly naughty, which is how he prefers to be naughty.

Tonight for him on video an adult woman with black hair, brown skin, brown eyes and a British accent, in ethereal black lingerie which she never removes, always teasing, teasing the camera and the man watching, she says "Stroke your cock, you loser," while loving how she knows the imagined watcher will love being called this and do such. She called Larry a loser and it's helping. He likes what's happening and considers this an erotic moment of personal discovery. *The Great Escape* sound stays running, the porn on low volume so his roommate, watching television down the hall in the living room, he won't hear neither the porn nor Larry masturbating.

"You cum diva, you bitch," she says to him, bending over, raising her skirt above her lace panties. She glares at the camera. She appears angry, frustrated. She describes how someone ought to be jerking off.

No question about it, Larry feels she understands him, and the two get along tremendously well.

Then on his computer he streams the Georges Delerue song "Générique" from the *Jules et Jim* soundtrack. He lies back for a moment, without a topic in his mind, without an emotion, for while "Générique" plays his worries are in a room separate from where he is now.

He experiences the tiny euphoria one feels after an orgasm, but no one sharing it with him, and with no one to whom he gave.

While "Le tourbillon" plays he feels nowhere but within the song. There's not a person in his room to surf with Larry the waves of Jeanne Moreau's voice.

He doesn't ask for his old moods to start coming back, for tired topics to reappear in his mind, but they come back to him on their own as they always do.

After "Jules et thérèse" ends he places *The Great Escape* on the 1hr40min mark again to quadruple-check the disc's status.

He finds it still skips.

Larry pauses the movie then again he chats with his Internet book friend right quick, this time hearing a story about the friend concocting a play, which play's script was handed to over twenty people by rough descriptions to each person for their character's intention, explained to them by the director Larry's friend, who performed the play and acted in it in the front lawn of a house.

The friend also added mini-details from his concurrent dalliance.

"This sounds like moments of the dream, wedged between other moments that sound outside the dream," Larry thinks of his friend's story.

Then he starts *The Great Escape* again at the beginning of the end part that doesn't skip, 2hr10min, closing his laptop and placing it on the wooden floor, lying down on his futon bed and knowing what he's done is he made it through another day.

Larry this night slumbers.

The writer astral hovers his imaginary body and whispers to the reader, since from the perspective of word planet the writer doesn't slumber and can astral hover.

Larry exists as the writer, but the writer doesn't exist as Larry. Larry Angeles is a movie that plays within the writer's head and which he adapts onto page. The emotional narrative vaguely reminds the writer of a self-help book compounded with a romanticised memoir, sprinkled with real philosophy, street style, similar to detective novels, New Age, graffiti, and this book sounds written from a character perspective personifiable by a domesticated animal disengaged from the room's tone but projecting certain ontological characteristics.

This is the writer's creation of Larry, his own Larry Angeles.

The backstory is Larry had pleaded for the writer to, "Tell a big story about a little person!" The writer had said, "Only if I can be honest." Larry had said, "Are you fucking kidding me if you ever aren't honest I'll lose my shit." Then, after the writer had said, "Honestly you're a little person who pretends losing his shit would be a big deal to anyone, seriously I mean you have big dreams and a tiny, bizarre life, with more ambitions than missions," they agreed on their plan. (Larry had locked imaginary eyes with the writer and through telepathy whispered, "Bring it.")

Their plan satisfies Larry since he desires for the world he fears to become more like words he adores.

The writer is a stern religious person about his personal conviction for words.

The writer attends churches for his personal beliefs.

Churches for people who worship words being books.

The writer learns from other writers their interior recipes, many of which have ingredients he didn't or couldn't find himself, and since the planet itself cannot talk with him, despite him sometimes thinking the great beauty of nature speaks, the writer reads a page then another, as he lives a day then another.

Books and people not only help him live but are why he lives.

This book is about that.

Larry as being described is both already made and being made. The writer doesn't even always feel in literal control of Larry, and the feeling is partially true regardless of being absurd. One Larry is the writer and one is the book, one isn't named Larry, and it's the writer's passion for this novella to twin his and their nature. The writing teleports onto word planet details from Larry's reality, resulting in methods from inner genre dimensions.

Both the writer and Larry have idiosyncratic philosophies, full personal perspectives, and invented intrinsics that mold them. The writer desires to retain how thorny Larry is as a person, while vacuuming thorniness from his prose (except leaving it when it feels right and projects qualities that Larry possesses), which is tricky-tricky, he writes one night to stress this point, then later he types: but if it isn't tricky it isn't risky, and if it isn't risky it isn't Larry-honest.

"Once on paper... this bothers me... I become altered by principles of word planet which, however brilliant, like adult planet, and science, I feel unable to control it controlling me," Larry says to himself in his dream he has, while riding a bicycle in the sky between two glass skyscrapers. "So, rational life pisses me off with its evidence of my imperfections, therefore I defy the adult planet's traditions by my own design, so in conclusion my natural course is to defy paper planet... I'll let science worry about science and I'll let me worry about myself," he hollers while twelve-speed pedaling through the troposphere.

Larry has perhaps a big picture to his life but mostly small pictures arrive to him now. He wants to throw them away, wishes he'd stop receiving them, here's a book about that too.

Later Larry will see friends. They do exist! There's going to be a work segment for categorical authenticity, there was already brouhaha about the street and the sun, which sun was clearly being used as a metaphor for the fear Larry has from the heat of other people's eyes, and yes the street is Larry, and the porn signifies that like Don Quixote his quest is for a lady to love, *The Great Escape* was random, and writing will be mentioned again later, since it's verifiable from these very words what writing means to Larry, and after Larry and the writer fuse and there's narrative methodicalness this book will end.

The writer's personal goal is self-awareness. He's using Larry for mental dialecticism, interpreting Larry's dream thesis, the antithesis of his reality, and the synthesis of his life as these words.

Here's a Fuck That toward writing in first-person, which feeling the writer has and I don't quite get him, and here's a personal story meant to arouse in the writer an emotional belief for words that he felt within back when as a teenager he watched *Caroline in the City* over an old cathode ray tube in his Bellbrook, Ohio bedroom.

Caroline (Lea Thompson) was seeing a guy who'd written a big book. She'd loaned the book to her comic strip colorist Richard (Malcolm Gets) to read and report back.

When asked about it later, Richard had read the book and said he loved it.

Caroline asked him what it was about.

"A horse kicks over a bucket," he said.

"What else?" she asked him.

"Well..." he said.

"It's 600 pages!" she said.

"I think it was a remarkable book about all of life," he said.

She stared at him.

◉◉◉◉◉◉◉◉

Waking in the morning alone on his futon is a terrible way to begin his day in Larry's opinion.

Going to sleep without someone to put your arms around and waking without someone's arms around you is a lonely and sad way to live this world. Plus, upon continuing to wonder when and how dreams come true, he's like, "Great, I had a nightmare." Plus, it's a damn futon. Is he still in his nightmare? This is a normal morning for Larry. He has zero missed calls. Zero texts. Zero plans outside of work. For several minutes after turning off his alarm he lies on his futon, not feeling awful so much as captivated by the concept of awfulness.

He has normal things to do in his normal life, which is not the life he wants nor can love today. He thinks, "Yesterday already happened."

Does he worry about the day behind him? No, that's already over. So he gets busy worrying about today.

From outside his trembling blue drapes come the rumbles and beeps of condo construction.

Larry momentarily feels with abundant clarity that he's a passenger on a boat of existence drifting from real meaning.

The plastic fan whirs. He rises, gathers together his clothes, takes a morning shower, brushes his teeth, grabs his work ID, thinks "What the fuck," walks two blocks toward work at the outdoor mall bookstore, ringing the bell when he arrives there and waiting to be let in, he's let into the building, then he clocks in and begins his work day.

◉◉◉◉◉◉◉◉

Larry is a bookseller, a.k.a. an unskilled laborer.

The job pays crap and it's a job teenagers handle, he got the job without a degree, with an expunged criminal record, a non-flattering resume, and his curios of personhood.

Today Larry is stationed where it's usual for him to be stationed, on the second floor, with its mezzanine of chairs for customers to read, and the large sections of movie, music, art, fashion and self-help books.

Plus wedding, psychology, cookbooks, and some other books but there's an outline.

For his first hour he shelves books, which keeps his time busy.

Sometimes customers ask him where a book is. Larry likes to hand a customer a book. He doesn't feel part of bigger things while working here, except for people liking to receive books he hands them, and people have the possibility of becoming a big deal.

This portion of adult planet cares if he shows up on time, works his hardest, smiles, shares a little story or bit of information, tells a joke, calls it a day.

Sometimes Larry does the obvious, sometimes he doesn't.

On occasion while he works, he wishes he were somewhere where he is someone whom he is not.

"This isn't who we thought it was," Larry think-says to himself about himself.

During days when he can't conquer his frustrations, on his irregular days of feeling irregular, there are days when he can't handle.

He tries to be the type of person who can be around people any day, including days when he isn't that type of person. But Larry is a bad liar. Some days he feels stuck falling down, down and people around him help bring him down, and he brings himself down.

Some days when he's down everything brings him down. He still shows up to work. There are the small moments and little smiles that lift him though his days, and there's word planet around him on shelves in the bookstore.

Word planet is familiar with human and inhuman topics from a kaleidoscopic spectrum spanning place and time. There he feels serene, visiting and/or vacationing perspectives outside his personal.

Larry tries, when he can and when he remembers, to pinpoint virtue outside rotten sensitivities his futureless, menial job affects in him when he lets it, since really he's not sure that's his biggest problem.

The writer would like to mention Larry has prominent features of the querulous subtype of a paranoid personality disorder.

He exhibits caviling, resentful, choleric, sullen, and waspish behavior.

He should see a psychoanalyst about this, a cognitive therapist perhaps, after he sees a general practitioner. He should see a dentist. He should buy new shirts. He struggles with knowing what about himself needs fixed and what he can and should fix. Larry wants to fix as little as possible and cherish everything as it is. He struggles with practical solutions. He should read Dale Carnegie and Julia Cameron.

Larry doesn't do what he should, he does what he does, and ultimately the world isn't as bad as it feels to him, so the writer whispers to him now, *Not everything is drama, Larry.*

Who knows what Larry learns and doesn't learn. Larry barely knows.

Since much of his life he spends stuck in his personal vision of his existence, interacting with his co-workers can soothe Larry.

He enjoys learning about his co-workers' lives and personalities. Sometimes there are petty dramas, cold shoulders, histories of misunderstanding and/ or general dislike. Sometimes his co-workers laugh with him, share emotions through stories, and/or things happen like maybe someone brought cheesecake into the break room.

He relates with his co-worker who has recently become fascinated by tarot cards, following his fascinations with bamboo massage, meditation and yoga. This co-worker quests through his life toward something to make him feel physically and emotionally accomplished in this world. Larry agrees with his quest, is fascinated by his fascinations.

He treasures his co-worker who dies her gray hair red and has strong, friendly opinions on a great many books and topics. One co-worker has a degree in Library Science and practices Wicca. She works at the Beverly Hills Public Library full-time. Many of Larry's co-workers have multiple jobs, since having a minimum-wage job in Los Angeles doesn't make one's life financially comfortable.

There's the bookseller who works this job, as an usher at Hollywood Bowl, a cashier at Whole Foods Market, and he's a guitarist and singer for a punk band, he used to only be a punk musician. Another bookseller, the ebook specialist, works here and at Universal Studios. Then another works here and at a pot dispensary (Xena cosplay sidestory). One bookseller went to clown college and also walks dogs, auditions for paid acting. A part-time children's department bookseller also works full-time for the city at a job that gives square pay and promises healthy retirement.

Larry used to work also as a furniture delivery person, now he works only here. Other people work only here as well, such as the lead in the music department, another of Larry's favorite co-workers, a born/bred Angeleno who has a strong affection for Germany, is learning about its culture and language, thinks he wants to maybe move to Germany, and also he thinks maybe he wants to go to college and major in Art History. The toys & games lead used to shoot videos for tourists on cruise ships, which while telling Larry this he smiled, said the job had its pleasures. He moved here to live with his brother and pursue careers directing in the movie entertainment business.

Another bookseller works here and performs standup comedy. A cafe lead (there's a cafe in the bookstore on the third floor) reads Bukowski on his breaks and has calm chats with Larry about topics such as being happy since that's better, since having this job is an obvious circumstance that could inspire a person to feel down, it isn't worth it, to let this place bring you down. Larry tries not to feel down here, and he achieves this minor victory in his life when he can.

Outside proper adults with unimpressive steady jobs, others arrive here straight from high school and are simultaneously taking their first college classes, and others transfer here from their home state. These types immediately declare this job as temporary.

The high school graduates are experiencing the adult planet for their first time. They're barely different from kids, they're both annoying and adorable. Some of the transfers are country kids moved into the big city, which Larry once was and he adores meeting others who are such. Some of them move into the city and kick a ton of ass at becoming who they want to become, immediately getting another and better job. They arrive as more badass than Larry and maintain themselves as such. Some don't find the city works for them, and they head back home or elsewhere.

Some of his co-workers are similar to Larry, feeling distant from their desires for themselves, surrounded by books every work day. Some co-workers, who might say they were born an alien, they don't care about books, don't read them, and while they work in a bookstore they idly wonder about their futures.

Some people have these qualities plus others, but they don't spend their time sweating small potatoes, they work here well and hard.

◎◎◎◎◎◎◎◎

"There are books and people," Larry thinks while facing the theatre book section from the second-floor staff table, then he turns and walks past sections for books on architecture, photography, interior design, crafts and hobbies, antiques and collectibles. He walks toward a window in the mezzanine that faces The Grove, a trolley rings its bell outside, then Larry turns to face the pet book shelves, searching for a book about dogs a customer had called to request holding for later purchase.

And for this, Larry currently makes a quarter over minimum wage, which raise of a quarter he obtained after a year's steady employment, after minimum wage itself had increased fifty cents. "The percentage to which I like and/or dislike this job is irrelevant to me needing stronger and sturdier financial security for myself through my adult years."

Larry longs for a better paying job he'll adore. He hopes to find it soon, whatever job it is. "How does someone get hired to write poems for neon signs, is that an artworld thing, I bet there's money there to be made for me and others from neon sign ideas I have, how about that, sassy universe," his emotions feel.

"Kids might desire to hang in their bedrooms crackling neon signs that say:

OPEN FOR BLISSES 24/7"

(There's currently no possibility of Larry being hired to write lines for neon signs, if that's even an available job.)

His bookstore job happened because his personal plan has been his bullshit life and he tries his best but he still fucks up. This is Los Angeles, 2015. This job arrived to him through a girl he was dating at the time, she worked here. She was nice to Larry and helped him through his life during a certain time to a specific degree. Then she told him she'd been serious when she was pushing him away and life's hilarious. She said this is life. She'd been making other plans for herself. In their final early-morning chat by the curb in her car, she told him she was thinking about herself for the first time in her life. She sounded liberated from Larry. He had such a long and dirty beard on his sad face then. From which she felt liberated. This had been February, when she called Larry backwards. She looked him in the eyes and in her eyes he saw her thrills dancing. Liberated. They haven't talked to each other in person since then.

According to this being written now, the reality of having intimacy shares a fundamental characteristic with the American dream, as for each the universal-positive angle is to say it's better for another person to experience romance and live their dreams, but lots of people have love, some people don't have lovers.

A few months from now Larry will have worked for two years at the bookstore where she helped him get a job. She left the store and was promoted in another job she works now. As an adult professional in an office she sees free movies and goes to the Oscars. In February Larry felt like his dreams, symbolized for a moment by her and movies, these were places where he'd never be.

Since her, he's single in this job he gave her.

He detects his need to remove himself from his situation.

Larry finds the dog book. It's a book about goldendoodles. Larry feels a little upset today but not too bad. The goldendoodle on the cover of the book relaxes him. He tells the customer over the phone that he put the book on hold. He mentions over the phone that the cover has a mellow goldendoodle, and the customer replies, "Of course."

⊚⊚⊚⊚⊚⊚⊚⊚

Larry visits the third-floor receiving room on occasion when he works the second floor.

There are things that happen, and things he will remember.

Such is Larry, things he knows and remembers and things he doesn't.

From the receiving room Larry might remember the rubber floor mats on the concrete, the musty smell of books and dust that sometimes caused him to sneeze, but will he remember the trash cans? Not likely, but he'll remember there were trash cans.

He wonders what from these eight-hour days he will remember. What he'll remember from each person he sees and hears across days and weeks.

He enjoys having chats with the receiving manager, who's also from Ohio.

Larry is easily seduced by Ohioans.

The manager has personal health complications, lives with his girlfriend's grandmother in Malibu, has written a script he hasn't yet wanted to tell Larry about, and Larry thinks this manager is a fine midwestern sample, one who doesn't need reminded neither how to be nice nor that life is hard sometimes.

The manager once said to Larry in a grim tone, "There's always something happening in life outside work, things going on that I don't talk about here."

Then he said something hilarious.

He's amiable. He works this job alongside Larry. Larry browses through books on H-carts ready to be shelved. He mentions to the receiving manager a little thing he notices, the title of a book, *"Everybody's Normal Till You Get to Know Them."*

Larry displays the book with the title he read, asking the manager if he also thinks the book's title is impressive.

The manager doesn't appear to want to think today about if he's impressed by the stupid book title or not. He might be though. His face says it. Larry notices. Larry hopes to raise his mood, so he goes on as he does as he always does, sharing his intrigue about a riddle of the human condition he notices being analyzed through cultural products.

"What's normal?! A classic question…"

"And… how you do get to know people?!?"

Perhaps Larry aims to share his findings with others for mutual benefit, perhaps he needs someone to make him feel less alone, there can be starvation in his eyes when he ferrets out conversations, or that and this and other reasons.

And more. Larry certainly searches for reason.

He shares pieces of his excitement from the world through conversations with others, including during moments when other people aren't in the mood to be excited about the easy, vulgar, and cheap poetics Larry adores. Now Larry bites his lower-lip and points his dumb-hopeful eyes at the receiving manager, waves to his not-yet-mentioned co-workers in the room, they too having heard about this book title he's been going on about owing to mischievous curiosity, then Larry smiles and elegant nods are shared and he concludes his one-sided conversation about the book ("It's Christian!") as he leaves the room, and after leaving the room he wonders what exactly of himself he left behind.

◎◎◎◎◎◎◎◎

There Larry goes living his life and thinking about it.

Life as big as what he thinks about and bigger too.

One could say Larry skis down reality's slopes.

Now he stands there and stares at his life, which is currently full of bookshelves and low pay. There in his Goodwill shirt, buttoned to its top, his black hair with its grey streak and its receding front, uncombed but by his hands, his weather-worn teeth, his troubled-times face, he's got a bit of a smile, he brushes his face with his hand and he thinks today has been a basic fuck of a day.

Sometimes while clocked in at the bookstore, after he's tidied shelves and placed books where they belong, or perhaps meanwhile, he stops for a moment to read the Internet on a work computer.

Usually a Wikipedia article about a writer or topic on his mind that day. Today on his mind is Don Carpenter, who wrote *Hard Rain Falling*, which Larry read, enjoyed, and considered realistic prose descriptions of a pool shark turned con turned ex-con. He found pleasure in reading the character's interesting life paths, and the narrative's footnoted affection for literature.

He'd thought of this book recently when he saw it on his bookshelf in his closet. Standing at the computer there and then Larry reads Don Carpenter committed suicide when he was sixty-four, after he'd been a professional writer for twenty-two years, including a stint in Hollywood, writing for example a 1977 screenplay titled *Charles Bukowski's Post Office*, which wasn't made into a movie. He wrote a 1972 movie titled *Payday*, which Larry has never heard of, so, this moment, related to him sometimes wishing he was not at work, and sometimes choosing not to work, along with growing affection for Carpenter and *Payday* the only linked title in Carpenter's Wikipedia writing credits, Larry clicks the underlined and blue-texted *Payday*, his curiosity beginning his Wikitrail.

Payday is about a traveling country-western musician who "gets himself into all sorts of adventures." It was filmed in and around Selma, Alabama. The actor who plays the musician is named Rip Torn. Larry likes the feeling the sound of this movie gives him. Don Carpenter was also a producer. The director Daryl Duke was from Vancouver, British Columbia. He was also the director of a well-known low-pitch crime movie co-written by Curtis Hanson, with Elliott Gould as a bank teller held up by a Santa Claus robber, *The Silent Partner*.

Then, while Larry is lost in thoughts that feel to him like simple surprises he discovers during his day at work, the punk rock bookkeeper rides down the escalator and notices another co-worker, a janitor, referred to as a porter on the daily assignment sheet, the porter pushes a wheeled plastic trash can in Larry's direction.

"Dinero fácil," the punk rock bookkeeper says, his current hair similar to Joe Perry's current hair, he points to Larry and shakes his head, his hair sways a little. The porter and bookkeeper laugh as the bookkeeper steps off the escalator. He pats the porter on the back and walks toward the next escalator.

The porter approaches Larry smiling. "Dinero fácil," the porter says. Larry wishes this meeting had occurred while he'd been working, and he sure feels busted. "Easy money," the porter says. Laughing. Larry laughs too, shakes his head also. The porter laughs and nods and smiles.

The porter pushes the trashcan toward the elevator next to Larry, who closes his computer window.

◉◉◉◉◉◉◉◉

At work on his first break Larry reads the reply text from his movie friend whom he had texted the evening before: *In San Diego until next week.*

Larry then reads *Factotum* at a cafe table on his phone. Later during his lunch break he reads the store's copy of *Factotum*. This book captivates him. Its style and personality, its wit and humor. He puts twenty pages in his memory pockets today.

Each day, at work and elsewhere, Larry jiggles in his memory pockets a book or books he's reading.

Walking through the store to clock back in from his lunch, Larry passes the C section of literature, picking up a book that has been serenading him, *Journey to the End of the Night.*

He reads again what appears to be an epigraph written by Céline:

"People, animals, cities, things, all are imagined. It's a novel, just a fictitious narrative."

This strikes Larry as an obvious book a guy like him should read. He puts *Journey to the End of the Night* on hold at work, then he thinks about it some more through his day, later he reads about Céline's personal life on Wikipedia, wishing he hadn't read that, but this book gains Larry's trust by referencing nighttime in its title, and by what he's read from it, and because he thinks he sees how it's a kernel within popular contemporary literature, and for other reasons, Larry tomorrow buys *Journey to the End of the Night.*

He brings it home for occupancy in his room on a stack with other books, next to other stacks. He intends to read *Journey to the End of the Night* when he can and does. He'll wait for days when it won't bother him to choose reading one long book over many other shorter books he wants to read and other things he has to do. When he craves the wide world of Céline's night he'll choose to travel there, he having taken such vacations into books before.

Larry, who hasn't had personal money for global travels, he travels the world through art. He's been to, for example, nineteenth-century Russia, where book people are prone to go, and Larry is aware that a person can become quite serious about surrounding life with words.

Regarding the topic of Larry's social characteristics while at work, which no one mentioned, he isn't splendid at finding reasons for conversation, but his best conversations feel natural and everyone gets along immediately.

The writer, while doing background research, discovered within Larry anecdotal descriptions of his interactions with customers:

"My personal experience demonstrates I get along best with international tourists, visitors from Italy or Poland or Costa Rica or Brazil or Russia or Japan."

"Since thinking outside the box can mean living or having lived somewhere else other than whichever place is describing the box, me here in Los Angeles, I think tourists think outside the box."

"Australians can be country friendly. A Kiwi can always tell you how a Kiwi is different. Snottiness doesn't come from places, it comes from types of people."

"Japanese people consistently have progressive, intriguing social characteristics, such as making small claps when hearing words that please them, and diverse and elastic personalities expressed through fashions across gender."

"I envy sun umbrellas."

"Also too I find rapture in Scandinavian culture and people from there, their strength through bleakness."

"Most women from India appear in marriages my dreams make."

"Though my dream depends on my day(?!?). The other day I saw a woman who was dressed in these terrific city clothes, black and white dance pants with decorative designs, a black jersey t-shirt with gold embossment, I found her style impressive and what I did, what I sometimes do in this type of situation, if I'm attempting to provoke conversation, I went over to her and told her I like her clothes, I asked her where she got them (since I want to dress the same), and she said she bought her garbs at Ross Dress for Less [which is across the street across from K-Mart], and she said she's visiting from Iran, I thought that sounded wonderful and we parted then, we both walked away and the world felt better to me, lighter. I like when I meet and get along with people whose personality invigorates me. There can be distinct value to a person's short burst in my life."

"Also I appreciate rebel-tender hearts from the American south, totally support Cascadia being founded, things like that."

❀❀❀❀❀❀❀❀❀

Description of a specific chapter within the twenty pages of *Factotum* that were read:

it was in italics, an irregular form not seen elsewhere in the book, a dreamlike memory from the dangerous world of drunken Hank (Bukowski), fighting with an old man at the tracks, Zsa Zsa Gabor on his mind, the old man being made to fall from the high seats, killed by Hank.

A particularly vibrant scene, this tightly sealed racetrack chamber drama, it's a tragic and poetic misstep from a person who more or less lived the city as he wrote it.

◎◎◎◎◎◎◎◎

Larry heads back to visit the receiving room manager again because it's today, Friday, and he can bring up movies opening this weekend.

It's summer. Multiplex movies are a more likely conversation topic for Larry with his co-workers, compared to books.

Ant-Man and *Trainwreck* are the Hollywood movies opening this weekend. Larry asks the receiving manager which movie he's looking forward to more than the other.

The receiving manager replies he can't say for sure, guesses he's about even.

Larry agrees with his perspective. Then the receiving manager, pepper in his voice, he does mention he did watch *Inside Amy Schumer*.

"Every episode?" Louise asks, emptying toys from a box onto a steel wheeled-cart.

"Every episode," the manager replies, scanning a book to put in a delivery box for a return to vendor.

Also *Irrational Man* is out, so there's a Woody Allen movie situation to consider, which Larry mentions while he glances around. The receiving manager flatly states, "I don't see Woody anymore." Present in the room is the receiving manager, Louise, Tony, Elizabeth and Larry. They create noises with their actions. A radio plays rock medium-quiet. The room smells like cardboard boxes.

"The last movie I saw and adored was *Tangerine*," Larry mentions. The manager smiles and nods while listening to Larry describe *Tangerine*, which Larry guessed no one in the room would have heard about, but he considers it a smashing movie and a fabulous conversational topic. He mentions being impressed by *Tangerine* playing in a serious LA movie theatre on Hollywood Boulevard after being shot on an iPhone 5S. "I saw it with my mom, and trans actors play trans characters," he exclaims for the room. Some people smile. Larry expresses his consideration of *Tangerine* as a benefit to both artistic and cinematic culture in America, since it shows cinema take digital form in an electric world vibrant with new cultural technologies. Though Larry's mother had noticed nothing but sadness, with hookers in a hotel room, a blowjob to a married man in a carwash, crack smoking in a bathroom, and emotional singing for but few others in audience that Christmas Eve. He couldn't convince his mother *Tangerine* was a beautiful movie, but she expanded his thoughts on its sadness.

That's what he calls a good movie.

Calibrating himself back to the room's tone, he tells the receiving manager this weekend he'd like to maybe theater hop from *Trainwreck* to *Ant-Man*. It excites Larry to feel excited about multiplex movies, which movies may or may not be exciting when he does or doesn't see them. Some of his thoughts about some movies he hasn't seen float as their reality to him.

The receiving manager nods.

Tony isn't listening.

Louise listens sometimes. He says "I downloaded *Ant-Man*," smiles.

Elizabeth left the room for her department.

Tony is about to leave.

Larry stares at books stacked on the table to be shelved. On top of the philosophy section he sees the illustrated book *Philosophy For Beginners*.

Tony departs.

Larry picks up *Philosophy For Beginners*, flips it open and reads from the book while the room is quiet. Philosophical ideas have dollar signs in his thoughts, regarding values he places on his inquiries into why he gets to live and what he can do about it.

It was Gramsci, the book tells him, who said everyone is a philosopher of sorts. Thales from Ancient Greece mentioned an aspect of philosophy that's been present since its beginning: the intended disentanglement of science from magic. Plato said there is "an ideal horse, outside space and time." Larry wonders about historic debates between science and magic regarding a horse's ideal form.

The receiving manager tells Louise he'll take out the trash before he leaves.

Louise says, "Okay."

While skimming the book Larry subconsciously considers if they're true the feelings that philosophy give him. They must be, but order and structure in philosophy come from hearing life.

A merchandise manager enters the receiving room.

The managers have a conversation about a Dodgers game the merchandise manager is going to. Listening to this conversation is the same for Larry as listening to the radio. Every now and then he does. "It's going to be sweet," is said.

"That's a great plan," he hears during their medleys of nods. A panoply of smiles are executed in regard to the Dodgers game.

Then Larry reads about Boethius, who in 5th Century CE, before the lights went out on philosophy for a thousand years, he wrote "Consultations of Philosophy" while in prison condemned to death by Emperor Theodoric, writing it was his guardian Philosophy who brought him "true happiness" before his death, which came to him shortly after.

Larry returns the book to its stack, thinking, "When I set this book down I return to my life..."

All of what happens through his life interests him. As he stares across the room at nothing, his vision blurred by his thoughts, his moods travel to France while he wonders, "Whom do I admire more, Charles Baudelaire or Jean-François Lyotard? Do I envy bringing electricity to art or electric descriptions of art? Stéphane Mallarmé or André Breton? Raoul Dufy or Camille Claudel? Are Simone de Beauvoir and Jean-Paul Sartre equal to me? Comte de Lautréamont or Albert Camus?"

"I have no idea."

"Only names, but people in life, with their concepts of reality."

"Alfred Jarry."

"There's so much to learn. There isn't too much. There's so much and there isn't enough. Everything I learn teaches me there's something else to learn."

"Being aware of this and learning more, have I gotten better? My whole life what I've wondered is how to live with others, which a lot of times is an unrelated topic to my problems except in hindsight."

The merchandise manager asks him what he's doing. Larry disengages from his personal mood, looks the manager in his eyes and says, "Keeping the second floor safe," turns to ask Louise when he gets off work, Louise glances at the clock and says "Sooon, three-thirty," then Larry pushes the handle of a V-cart out the room for shelving, stopping by the information desk to grab a pile of books customers had left behind on cafe tables.

Larry's life philosophy operates on the principle that a person shouldn't carry beliefs due to their personality-warping features.

To him beliefs give people hang-ups and place pressures and burdens on their perspectives. He wonders/hopes if not believing anything allows what happens to become anything it wants to become. He'd live a holy life he discovered through a philosophy which perfectly suits him, but since he hasn't encountered such a philosophy yet, including a philosophy of not having a philosophy, he continues living regardless.

Larry is aware he exists past post-structuralism as everyone does, in a world self-aware of its own enormity, aware of its global infrastructure, and its imperfections, among the total mass of recorded years, people, and ideals. A theory of everything is a current goal in physics. Larry is fascinated by model-dependent realism. This shares cosmogonic qualities with epistemology, which also has meta-epistemology, also constructivist epistemology and more. Perennial philosophy is being listed as a religion.

That's a soft push into a big picture. There are multiple big pictures. (For aesthetics, the writer will say one leads by example.) Point is, the world today is larger than anyone guessed it would be, so everyone is trying to think about what to do. Larry agrees. There's an intensity to this, owing to the digital age of information. Today's names and ideals become yesterday's, we all know that, and we all know we all know that because of modernity, which, modernity, doesn't mean what it used to.

We definitely means more than it used to.

In this melodramatic allegory a person chooses a life philosophy:

She bought a Tesla because of course she bought one. She supports alternative energies and clean air. Also she supports having a new car. She bought the Model S, nineteen-inch black matte wheels.

She cruises in style and enjoys having made her choice.

Then there arrives Tesla's Model X. Its doors are better. Its doors are more impressive. It has falcon wing doors, and that's a slick new feature that becomes a status symbol.

Upon the Model X arriving she begins to worry about her Model S. The Model X becomes popular in her region. It becomes more popular than the Model S. Though her Model S suits her well, with it she doesn't feel unique or view herself as a trendsetter, instead now she feels utterly in the past. Her having money to buy this car, she doesn't every day treasure her Model S itself, no, and she doesn't wish her Model S was a Model X, she wishes her car was a Model Y and that she had it before anyone else.

❖❖❖❖❖❖❖❖

Larry always hopes that when he discovers what he cannot guess he finds something that's transformative or interesting.

Or at least weird as fuck, at the bare minimum.

He idealizes newness and change. Which results in him making mistakes, of the artistic and living variety. Not everything new to Larry is progress. What's new to him can be history when he finds it. It can be bad news when he creates it. It can be something else.

He jiggles regrets in his memory pockets, but he lives committed to self-forgiveness for mistakes that on his worst days make him wish he didn't exist. It'd be easier for him not to exist, he's thought before. He attempts to remain aware that life is not just what's easy, and often the problem with the easy is it feels too easy. He asked the writer to say the following: "I want to live a life that's thought about. I want to think a life that's lived. I want both and neither. My life itself feels to me like a double bind… risky by its nature, and I don't not worry about anything.

"Longing to see the world better-better, art motivates me to better see the world, but the problem can be I then search not for more life, but for more art, and art becomes an illusion of life I practice… that's better… but what I want is better-better."

"Then I do what I do because that's what I do."

Larry, after his presentation was performed by the writer, for which Larry clapped, then he remembers having also heard people say, referring to perhaps a book or a movie or a song, that a cultural item made the person feel how the person didn't feel before. It having changed their feelings, it changed them. He remembers art brings different changes to different people, if it brings to them anything at all.

Larry has never read a book he's liked more than a person.

But he's more familiar with reading books than meeting people.

(He does like some books more than some people.)

He's spent more time reading than vacationing.

He knows word planet better than he knows planet Earth.

It's helpful to him that he views art as at least equal to reality.

He thinks both art and reality are determined by people.

With both art and reality it's one's memories which are the scale.

The lesson Larry carries into his world from books and movies is art's purpose isn't to be the world, but to show it, and he can see with his eyes the meaning of art in his world.

Larry spends much of his time thinking about his own perspective, his own experience with words and his own life's memories.

Nope, that's not where everyone else's thoughts are.

A misfortune of Larry's moods is they have the potential to launch his thoughts into stratospheres inappropriate for select conversations, which blunders he then makes, upon reflection, result in him noticing a fact along with him being an idiot.

From his experiences of being right and wrong, Larry thinks what's important after a disagreement is each person walks away in high spirits for their future battles with this world. He doesn't often reach what's important. He doesn't always know what the facts should be (that's a flex problem), and he can't always differentiate between when he's being brave and when he's being emotional and/or incorrect.

Finding disagreement with many people over many things, he chances upon harmony with others through shared curiosities and excitements, which are childish qualities on adult planet. On adult planet knowing an answer is preferred over looking for one. It's a fact that it's better to have facts and he doesn't disagree with this principle. There are facts he has and facts he doesn't have. He mentions this. And everything makes him curious, that's a Larry fact. He's mad curious about what he doesn't know, and he's even more curious about what exactly he needs to know.

Most experts of many crafts which require skill reach the peaks of their talents through rigorous practice, and Larry is interested in using this technique to become skilled at living.

He's neither fully rational nor fully irrational, though he desires to be full of each.

Larry knows, feels that the universe doesn't care what he knows, feels.

He's relatable, he's absurd, he feels inconsequential and he wants always to be how he is not. Which, by the way, made humans bring themselves to how they are now, in terms of skyscrapers and planning trips to Mars, et cetera.

And Larry is familiar with what's heavy, what's a bummer, and what can sink a person. His frustrations weigh down his living, since the foundation for his personality is his life experience, and Larry can forgets that neither he nor his personal ideals are the foundation for this planet.

His frustrations affect his life in ways altered both by how he feels and whom he's around and how that person feels. Larry, who is often alone anyway, he has regrets but he doesn't have shame, thinking solitude is regret's playground and no one needs shame in a playground.

On his strong days he remembers his thoughts aren't reality and his problems aren't a big deal and he doesn't sweat nothing. Those are the days when he both lives better and reads better. The good days come in phases like the bad ones. In a long good phase his better feelings accumulate, his thoughts can feel highly calibrated, and he can reach a mood that makes him feel as if he's seeing better. But there's always another feeling after the best. Always another way to see gets seen. In a long bad phase Larry feels the accretion of bullshit from himself and others.

The good and the bad conflate in him on his ritual days, which means he often feels he hopes for the best and accepts the worst.

◉◉◉◉◉◉◉◉

Dialogue from when Larry is paged to work as a cashier during his shift:

"I wonder what it'd be like to be a mom. There are female writers now, you know, who write about specific female topics..."

"Yeah..."

"Yeah, and recently I heard about the book *I Just Want to Pee Alone*. I felt philosophically sympathetic to the title."

"There's a word for it... I forget the word for a mother thinking and worrying about her kid when she's in the shower."

"You can't even shower without thinking about your kid?"

"Exactly. I listen for my kid when I'm in the shower, think about my kid at night before I sleep. I bet your mother worries about you."

"She does. So not only is it difficult to be physically alone, but psychologically alone. You're helping me think about this more."

"Yeah. Well, I've heard that book title maybe. Maybe I'll read it. I'm a mom, and it's comforting to hear from other moms about being a mom. The number of things you go through in a day, all the things, they can make you feel insane. Until you read about someone else, then you don't feel alone with your fights that make you feel insane."

"Isn't that the purpose of art, to make a person feel less alone in this world? And I like how contemporary art is made with direct relatability for specific types of people."

"Yeah."

"Do you want to buy a bag for a dime?"

"No thanks."

"Cool. Here are your books."

"Thanks."

"Thank you. I didn't know I'd have this conversation today."

"Neither did I," she says as she smiles and he smiles and she walks away.

◉◉◉◉◉◉◉◉

"I wouldn't read a story about me written by someone else," are Larry's subconscious thoughts on this topic, as he shelves self-improvement books on the second floor against the wall. The marriage section to his left. The medicine section behind him. Psychology behind it. Health and fitness behind it. Fashion to the left.

Larry's subconscious thinks, "There are fiction writers who could write my flaws from a direction I hadn't considered. Easy. Other writers could have novel ideas about what's the matter with me, including from their personal experiences and observations, scientific discoveries they've read about, social revelations they're clued into, and health benefits that are self-evident."

Larry, full of problems, in his regular life routines he learns he's having the wrong problems according to others. Not just superficially, but fundamentally, spiritually. Subtextual problems exist within him. He knows of them though he can't name them.

He wouldn't read about himself from a perspective that doesn't encourage him to live without fear and for shared good with others.

On the third floor, where Larry walks now, nearby fiction is poetry, nearby which are the philosophy and religion sections. Also mystery, sci-fi, graphic novels, manga, teen novels, travel books, tarot cards, astrology, and libros en Español.

Past business and nature and science, on the other side of the third floor sports are next to parenting. There's also humor and trivia, and the bargain section adjacent to the event space where celebrities and people considering feeling like celebrities visit to sign their books. As journalism from 2015 mentions, and as they love, love to mention themselves, it's the YouTube stars who are awarded the highest hysterias. Tears and screams happen. Celebrities on their way to the bathroom are chased by guys and girls. While they're in the bathroom, today's YouTube celebrities know people stand outside anticipating the star leaving the bathroom.

Larry at the bookstore as the bookstore, back in the fiction section. He earlier mentioned he wouldn't read about his life as written by someone else, but he was exaggerating. The writer is calling his bluff. Larry was having paranoid fears about how others may see him, though he would indeed read about his life if written by a Spanish-language writer for example. A writer who knows how to treat a person with words. For example (this is only one example!), Enrique Vila-Matas. To demonstrate why, the very first line to his *Never Any End to Paris*: "I went to Key West in Florida this year to enter the annual Ernest Hemingway look-alike contest." This person is familiar with people and word planet. Larry thinks Spanish-language writers possess capabilities of verbal precision from their personal devotion to the cause of literature. Javier Marías. Gonçalo Tavares. Sergio Pitol. Javier Cercas. Horacio Castellanos Moya. Alejandro Zambra. César Aira... Larry desires to use the concept of flight forward from inner genre dimensions.

"In Larry Angeles, Tod Browning's basement will have a diner named Nunca Duerme, and its interior design will be reminiscent of set designs from movies directed by Pedro Almodóvar."

"Atop Tod Browning, which is mostly five stories, except not really because a column, named Adolfo Bioy Casares, abruptly protrudes from its roof's center, and when the column has risen to the height of one-hundred stories there's a bowling alley that's larger than Tod Browning, named The Bug, it spreads itself out into the sky as a principal form of shade for this region."

"Everyone here will know The Bug."

Larry's moods can't always mirror his reality, and on his worst days his moods are barely similar to his reality.

69

Which he thinks is bogus.

His dreams and his reality are equal in his memories, but Larry has intense curiosity about what his future reality will be, and his reality of yesterday means more to the adult planet than his dreams.

Larry, unsure of both his dreams and his reality, considers himself a person whose soul is composed as a question mark, with his life as the dot. He also thinks, "Life is cinema, we're in the audience together, we're on the screen together, not everyone likes the movie but everyone watches, except also some people fall asleep or leave or never arrive, yeah," his thoughts have said [kidding].

Desires and appetites for art from books music and movies brought Larry to Los Angeles. He wants never to let them fall from his thoughts, he hopes to create his dreams from his hands, fearing himself becoming a person who arrived in Los Angeles with a dream for his life which over the years drifts further and further from his reality.

Though it's not by worrying about himself through which his life finds forward momentum, nor through worries others have of him, but through what he does and how he lives.

His is not a dishonest life of perfection, but an honest life of several mistakes

✿❀✿❀✿❀✿❀✿

Speculative breakdown of Larry's customary work thoughts, helpful for this book about him that's basically listerary autofiction a.k.a. creative nonfiction:

2% urban planning for Larry Angeles

4% inactive

7% (lucky number) disinterested rationality toward being a bookseller

13% (backup luck) his current moment

17% displaced considerations acquired from movies, music, or recently consumed books

18% people who interest him and what certain people mean to him

19% what he wants to write

20% what he wishes life was for himself and others

Larry, does life frighten him?

It has before, and because it has before he worries it will again.

Then, Larry is he strong, and from where does his strength come?

He's thought about this.

■■■■■■■■■

Larry has allowed his thoughts to wander off from the writer who was listening.

To repeat: Larry's thoughts have wandered off from the writer, though Larry is still at his job in the bookstore, and it's the damndest thing.

It's happening and it can't be and it's happening.

◼◻◼◻◼◻◼◻◼◻

Larry appears similar to Mina in the writer's imagination now.

Mina in Jafar Panahi's *The Mirror*.

Mina, finding her way home from school after her mother failed to pick her up, she flees from the camera filming this as her movie, in order to live her life (which continues to be her movie).

Larry had told the writer he's going to concentrate for a little while. The writer could've trimmed this entire section into the phrase, "Larry masquerades his neurotic labyrinth while at work," the writer could have said that and only that but he didn't, he did what he's doing.

Larry has to be himself. The writer feels the same.

Larry now makes a face as if concentrating on work. He lets himself appear dedicated to the mission of helping a person find a book.

Whatever. The writer doesn't know what Larry thinks now, outside of being familiar with the general list of topics in his normal and basic work thoughts. To not play along with his game, the writer would like to mention he doesn't care what the hell the specifics to Larry's thoughts are.

The writer currently doesn't care if Larry exists or not.

Larry could die right now, who gives a fuck?

Now the writer thinks about whatever the hell the writer wants to, and the topic sure as shit isn't Larry.

"Whatever and die yourself." Larry lets this thought broadcast from himself to the writer.

Apparently the writer remains in Larry's thoughts, even when Larry feels his worst.

Well, well, well.

Larry is something. Then he gathers a stack of books from the table and carries them for reshelving. When he kneels in the drama section to shelve Sam Shepard's *Fool for Love*, he makes a particular face then. The writer sees it. The writer knows this face. The writer knows that Larry knows what's he doing, and he wants out of this as well. His face meant, "We can get out of this if we want to."

The writer waits a moment. The writer thinks about something definitely not Larry.

For the writer it's November seventeen, three-oh-three pm. Work is at four.

Larry's day (mentioning), is July ten. It's also three-oh-three pm for Larry, who works until six.

Larry sighs, rolls his eyes. Winks.

The writer can't believe that Larry winked at him.

Outrageous.

Larry is such a fucking goose who thinks he's a prince.

Alright. Larry, right now, is a pissy attitude.

Larry stands akimbo and shakes his head.

The writer doesn't give a fuck.

You wouldn't believe the amount of sass in Larry's akimbo.

The writer would like to mention a gazebo.

The writer secretly gives a fuck.

The writer would like to move forward and so would Larry, so they do.

◉◉◉◉◉◉◉◉

Dialogue from when Larry is paged to work as a cashier again:

"I'll be standing here, no one around, then suddenly a long line of people appear together all at once from nowhere."

"It's the herd mentality. It's humans drifting toward others through not wanting to be alone," and during this transaction Larry thinks he's heard before about aspects of register lines echoing aspects of herd mentality, but he preferred how she said it.

Larry says there's something else he'd like the writer to mention.

Sure.

It's being mentioned that Larry reminds himself of Matti Pellonpää in *Shadows in Paradise* and *La Vie de Bohème*, as he thinks he's strong the ways in which he is.

He's strong enough to get through his days. He lives the hard life (without success or intimacy) as well as one can (without dying).

Larry tries to remember it'll be just one day that's the day he dies.

◎◎◎◎◎◎◎◎

He closes the computer's browser window when the store manager walks toward him.

She's dressed sharp, every day she is, and also every day she's serious about being the manager of this store, she's stern, she's nice once you get to know her and once she knows she can control you.

Larry looks like an idiot. She stares at his navy Vlado Milo Canvas shoes, which are high-top sneakers with brown heel indentations.

She frowns. "You've had," she holds up two fingers, "two complaints."

She makes a face. She looks at him, right in his eyes: "Is there something going on?"

He asks, "What were the complaints?" He wonders who ratted him out as a bad person and why, he says, "I feel fine, everything's fine, thanks."

The store manager looks at Larry like she doesn't believe him. He relates to her look. What will happen, he wonders. A customer comes to the staff table to ask about a book. He responds to the customer. The manager leaves. He helps the customer, then he goes to straighten some books on some shelves. He returns books to where they belong. He helps another person or three find a book. He calls the store manager to say he's going on his break. He reads on his phone articles about scifaiku and microaggressions. He checks out NatGeo's main page. Then he works again, arranging more books on shelves, walking people to books. He jaunts the third floor once, twice. His eyes comb the covers of new releases. He enjoys reading the dedications and epigraphs and first lines of books. He goes to the first floor and strolls through the movie department. He browses for the oldest and wildest. He wonders if he should buy *Meteor* on blu-ray. A lady approaches him and says her niece from West Virginia is amazed by the size of this bookstore. "She's never seen anything quite like this. She's seen two floors, never three." His work shift ends, he walks straight back home, and inside his apartment he grabs his blu-ray of *The Great Escape*.

He dumps *The Great Escape* on a filled trash bin on the corner of Fairfax and Oakwood. He sets it faceup on top, in case anyone for any reason wants to grab a blu-cay copy of *The Great Escape* resting on a trashcan in Los Angeles, and what he thinks now is, "Wish I still owned that movie, damn."

⊙⊙⊙⊙⊙⊙⊙⊙

Larry buys a Snickers Peanut Butter Squared from the gas station.

It's after 6, Ricardo is cashier. He's a bearded, friendly person, an Army vet with a kid, he once asked Larry to check if the bookstore had *Solitary Fitness* by Charles Bronson, which sadly it did not.

Then Larry returns to his apartment (after briefly sauntering in his back alley). Then moments occur through his life that aren't being mentioned, concluding with Larry walking across Oakwood to his old friend's apartment.

This old friend is in a relationship with Larry. He's one of the only friends

Larry has in the world, a person with whom Larry has shared much of his life, and there is pretty much something kind of romantic about them, for example their earlier-mentioned teenaged-rides through the backroads of Ohio.

Bless.

Often if Larry is headed someplace it's to his old friend's place.

Larry, now in his old friend's living room, his roommate the poet there, the poet checks his phone, an Etta James record plays, and Larry stares at the television, which rests on a menu screen for the videogame *Splatoon*.

Larry's old friend concludes doing something in the kitchen which involved clattering, before returning to the living room and sitting on the couch next to Larry.

"Sorry about last night," the old friend says to Larry. Larry nods and smiles. "Did you go anyway?" the old friend asks, referring to the Tao Lin and Mira Gonzalez discussion of *Selected Tweets*.

The poet looks up, he and his old friend watch Larry, wondering how his head will shake. His head shakes no.

Larry tells them, "I went home, read for a little bit, fiddled around on the Internet, then finished watching *The Great Escape*, went to sleep. That's it."

"Pretty good night," the poet says as he puts away his phone.

◎◎◎◎◎◎◎◎

Feeling they live on a planet that doesn't dream of them as they dream of it, at least in this room these three feel better while around each other.

It's in the feels where Larry and his friends live.

The old friend turns his head toward his orange-and-white cat sitting on the edge of the couch, and he asks his cat, "Oh man oh man, Gus. Is life a drag or a dream?"

His old friend nods as he begins blowtorching his dab rig. After the rig is red he places down his blowtorch, presses wax against a domeless nail, then he inhales.

"You still working on your novella?" the poet asks Larry.

Larry, while eagerly nodding, tells them both, "What's exciting to me is this one, I'll finish it. I feel I'm being brave how I can be brave." The old friend makes a slight cough related to exhaling his dab. "I think I'll finish this one and have finally finished a novella. I've said I wanted to do this since before Long Beach, West Tenth Street... those early days... since before then... me alone in my bedroom in my mother's apartment in Laguna Niguel, writing poems for you and Richard to read," he says while pointing and smiling at his old friend, who smiles too, "back when I wrote a short story for a book of shorts I wanted to finish and title *Man, Etc.*, but I haven't yet finished a book so I'm against some of my past life choices... I, I plan to make things better now, and this is when I say I'll do that then have done it."

The old friend says, "Doing it," as he motions to concentrated wax on a pick. Larry nods and scoots forward. Larry says, "In my novella there's been some walking around, it's based on how I picture my life through words." His old friend hands Larry the waxed pick.

His old friend ignites the blowtorch and heats the domeless nail. "Not much has happened... which makes it realistic to my current days," Larry says as the domeless nail heats to red and his old friend backs away from the rig.

Larry places the wax against the domeless nail. He inhales. He waits a moment. Then he exhales, loudly coughs. He stands and walks around, coughing.

Larry coughs again, then turns back around to his friends. "I'll probably include this conversation in the novella." His old friend smiles. The poet looks at his phone. "This interaction with us will be in the novella?" the poet asks. Larry nods. "Sounds boring," the poet says. Larry laughs. "I'm not worried about whether it'll be boring," Larry says.

"I'm worried about whether it'll be honest or not," Larry says. He paces. His excitement takes escalators up his feelings while he's high. "I think it's as honest about me as it can be, and it'll be something I can only write in two thousand fifteen as the person I am now, you know..." Larry mentions to them, except his old friend has left the room again, gone down the hall to his bedroom, so Larry told the poet.

"I want to read you something," the poet says. "I've got pieces written with about seventeen thousand and twenty thousand words each, and they could maybe be put together."

"You're going to be able to finish a novella no problem," Larry tells the poet.

"Or, are you thinking novel?"

"I'm thinking novel," the poet says.

Larry thinks, "My life is space junk in the universe, I sift through my trash, I compress my trash into words," then Larry thinks something else and he looks at his empty hands, his thoughts ride escalators in his feelings, then the poet begins to read from his phone a story he wrote about visiting the apartment of a work-friend of his, a middle-aged man who spoke Spanish around the poet. The poet spoke Spanish while quoting his co-worker, and in the story and through his voice it's clear the poet enjoyed learning about his work-friend's personality from drinking beer with him.

Larry vibes with the poet's enthusiasm for time spent with other people.

He enjoys hearing his poet friend's story.

The reading lasts a couple minutes.

At the end of his reading, the friend apologizes for having read for so long. "I didn't mind," Larry says, and he hadn't minded. He wanted to hear about the co-worker and hear the words his poet friend had used to write.

He knows he needs to be in this room around people whose lives are separate from his own.

The poet thanks Larry again for listening.

The Etta James record has finished, the poet had flipped it, both sides are concluded. He asks Larry, "Anything you want to hear?" and Larry replies, "Oh, I don't know, anything…"

Blondie's *Eat to the Beat* plays in the room. The poet sits in a chair. Larry's old friend is back from his bedroom, sitting on his couch smoking a cigarette.

Larry feels better now than he did before.

He doesn't feel happy but he doesn't feel terrible, which is as good as he knows how to feel these days.

Larry springs(!) from the couch and paces the apartment.

"Good, bad or whatever my life is, I share it with these two people, they're my emotional perimeter, they're two of the few people who care about me in this world. I hope they'll read my book, but I can't really worry if they will, since indeed they're more important to me than my words," say his subconscious feelings while taking surreal elevators in abnormal places.

He looks at his old friend on the couch. His old friend has been talking, now stares at him. "I'm sorry, my thoughts were pacing. What'd you say?" Larry says.

His old friend stares at him with intense eyes.

"Unbelievable," his old friend says, then he lights another cigarette.

"That's my bad," Larry says. "My thoughts were..."

"You didn't hear a word of what I said?" his old friend asks.

Larry shrugs, shakes his head no.

The room turns icy quiet.

Larry realizes now the poet is no longer in the room.

It's a room with only Larry and his old friend, who's been talking without being heard.

Larry doesn't like the sound of himself here now, as he thinks, "People need each other! People need each other and should be present for each other, absolutely. That's a truth that needs to be revered..."

"Furthermore, I'm not certain there are other people in this world who want to be with me more than these two people, who are my friends," his feelings yell while riding up an escalator.

His feelings have spotted a lesson. Always listen to others. His moods are going to install this lesson in his life, and he hopes not to create this uncomfortable situation between himself and someone else again in the future.

"Did you hear me this time?" his old friend asks him.

Larry stares at his empty hands.

"You didn't, did you?" his friend asks, staring at him, not with shock in his eyes, not with utter resentment, but with traces of repugnance. "Do you remember how to be around people, Larry?" his old friend asks. "You don't remember how to be social anymore, do you?"

Larry's not sure he remembers such things, but he often wishes he did, he often wishes he knew better how to be around people, how to make the world feel better for himself and others, and he wishes this while in this room now.

◉◉◉◉◉◉◉◉

Then arrives symphonic silence.

People Larry adores, he pushes them from himself with his personal overabundance.

He often overwhelms a room by overwhelming himself.

Often. Not comfortable with himself, he isn't comfortable with others. And being uncomfortable with neither himself nor others, people are prone toward feeling uncomfortable around him, which increases his and their personal discomfort.

He stares back at his old friend and says, "I don't know what's going on. Are you upset? What did you say?"

"Well, I already repeated myself," his old friend says while shaking his head.

Silence arrives that can shove a person. Silence shoves Larry.

Larry would be more worried if his thoughts weren't riding escalators.

"I don't feel comfortable," Larry says, staring at his hands again, then staring out the window just to stare out the window.

"You're having one of your things again," the old friend says.

"I'm listening. Can you... will you repeat it again? This is my bad," Larry says.

His eyes are locked with his old friend's.

He can tell he's done for. Blown it.

◉◉◉◉◉◉◉◉

Back in his apartment, squirming in his loneliness, wondering who cares, worrying about the troubles he has that he doesn't want, Larry lies still on his futon bed.

He can't exactly calibrate this particular night of his.

It's eight-forty p.m.

He doesn't want to sleep until midnight. He doesn't work tomorrow until the afternoon.

He desires to relish his time off work, this night of his, his life.

He lies there, keeps lying there, then his eyes close. After several long minutes, while he does nothing, and while he can think of nothing to do, another day ends and Larry falls asleep, bringing himself closer to his death.

There asleep on his futon time clicks on.

Time oblivious to Larry.

He should learn far better ways to care about time, but time doesn't now nor ever will it care about Larry.

He jolts awake at four-fifteen a.m., for no apparent reason, but now he's bummed he hadn't brushed his teeth.

Keeping the lights off so they don't shine on his eyes, he sits on the toilet lid and brushes his teeth, wanting to lie back on his futon bed and sleep for his next day.

He hopes there's a day coming for him that's different from his recent days.

Larry hopes for a new day to begin a new path that'll lead him to a new life.

"Let such events occur," he quietly dreams on the toilet while brushing his teeth in darkness.

"Except a new life doesn't come after a single day of nothing..." he ruefully remembers as he spits in the white porcelain sink. Then there he is again back on his futon, his eyes closed, sleep having been waiting for him.

◻◻◻◻◻◻◻◻◻

Now it's the end of another tomorrow.

There's an eggshell blue typewriter in his bedroom, though Larry writes on his silver finished laptop, and there's an unplugged record player on his floor but he streams Tom Waits for atmosphere.

He writes reclined on his green shag rug, slouched against his blue futon. The futon is in the room's middle, on the other side a dirty red shag in front of this room's door. The walls are nothing but white paint. Stacks of books rest next to the television facing the futon on a stand next to the windows. Odors of days gone by drift from soiled clothes in a corner next to a closet, the closet has two shelves of books, and books rest in a bookshelf next to the closet, and discs with movies live on shelves next to the door and on another shelf in another corner by the windows.

Owing to logistics, since in this book the writer creates Larry, direct and pure overlap between Larry writing and living happens when in the narrative Larry writes.

As is happening now.

Larry composes himself with words he gives the computer.

While writing and checking his writing, Larry finds he agrees with himself on most issues.

These words aren't his life, his life isn't words. His thoughts aren't reality, it's true. So his thoughts not like what he knows is reality, how then can he expect anyone to be like him?

Larry, while he lives while he writes, he realizes he doesn't have to concentrate to be weird, he requires serious concentration for normalness.

The normal terrify him, and that terrifies him, and he wonders what normal sees when it sees him.

And now he wonders: how will he disengage from himself in order to better see other people's realities? How will he better know the senses of others and continue to better know his own?

He wonders about this and that and other things. He wonders too about time, his life, life and time in general as reality, and the time it takes to get to know other people in a reality that's larger than them as well.

■■■■■■■■■

Still that night, now Larry toplessly writes his book in his briefs and without socks, shaking his ankle-crossed feet.

Daft Punk's "Something About Us" streams.

From a window in his thoughts floats into his room a dove. This dove circles the ceiling and makes soft coos. A top hat shoots out of the chimney that manifests itself in his closet, the top hat floats across the room and lands in Larry's hand, and as he reaches toward the dove she flies inside the top hat and enters its void. Larry puts the top hat on his head and writes on his laptop, he's excited, per the laws of being himself. He hears the dove cooing from the void.

(He'll write the dove from out of the void into which he put it, because he knows he must.)

◉◉◉◘◉◉◘◉◉

Both Larry and the writer exist as written, both could use a redraft, but Larry is in fact the only one who gets a redraft, the writer gets more days, and they both have a final draft.

The first draft of this book was far more depressing.

The bad in this book feels in fact worse in reality from certain perspectives, except reality is better by virtue of fact being better than fiction. Though still, the writer and Larry hope words and Larry deserve each other and their union makes them each stronger. Now hands fall off clocks, Larry thinks about things he's done, wonders why he did them, types on his laptop. He types, "Why does this section exist and what's the purpose?" He continues thinking, "...questions that can be applied to this narrative can be applied to my life."

 Now it's another morning before another day of work. It's Sunday. Larry is tired. He works soon. Sunlight kisses the wall and floor, gushing from outside the edges of his royal blue curtains which tremble from a light wind, a baby blue Old Navy t-shirt dangles and sways from a white plastic hanger on a black curtain rod, his fan whirs, Courtney Barnett's "Pedestrian at Best" streams.

All of humanity can relate to Larry in the present, based on the Theory of Everything not being cracked yet, and some people work on that and some people work on other things, and most people have their own personal abysses beneath them, and work keeps happening and days keep happening and it all keeps happening.

It's a scientific fact that the happening never stops.

Larry neither has a kid now nor plans for one soon. He has instituted methods of artistic procreation. What he can say about this book is he likes to be around it.

About Larry's senses, his reality, and science, Larry in fact wishes he existed only in words.

◉◉◉◼◉◉◼◉◉

Larry now writes how he wants now to leave his room, then he does both those things, air blue suede adidas gazelle shoes installed on his feet, he gathers together his wallet, phone and keys.

He paces his bedroom for a moment, briefly considering some things agitating him recently, reflecting on mistakes he's made through the week, and contemplating things he might do soon. Construction noises enter his open windows, quiet traffic noises float from Fairfax.

◉◉◉◉◉◉◉◉

Then walking down Beverly in the evening after work, Larry passes the Taschen Building and thinks, then he keeps thinking, he keeps walking, then Sunday passes by him, then it's Monday and he passes by the Taschen Building again, at night after he worked again, same thing different day, except this night he reads Valeria Luiselli's *Faces in the Crowd*, then it's Tuesday, then it's Wednesday morning, then it's afternoon.

◉◉◉◼◉◉◼◉◉

Wednesday afternoon: Larry in his apartment's living room he sits on his roommate's reclined chair, his laptop perched across his inner thighs, he wears gray insulation-themed joggers, the black plastic fan whirls, some sweat streams down his face.

Los Angeles is quiet, except a leaf blower yells out its heart from next door. Larry streams Soko's *My Dreams Dictate My Reality*. He feels as if his right now isn't a big drama and his worries are outside this moment. He escapes from this world into his skull-sized kingdom. He types the best he can and he takes the shape he has within the universe.

He looks in the madness and there he is.

He's in the madness and he's part of it.

"*Live Anyway, Write Anyway*, that'll be the motto of the Larry Angeles Book Club, which will have the character and reputation of a martial arts school."

◉◉◉◉◉◉◉◉

The sun slaps him as he strolls across Oakwood sidewalks, taking it easy.

It's Thursday, a week from the narrative's start, this ending like its beginning. Then tentacles reach from the sky and fling Larry through galaxies toward a planet inhabited by one woman, who keeps her one friend, a red rose, under a glass case.

Larry splats dead next to the woman on her planet, having smashed her red rose in its glass case with his dumb body, his eyes having popped from his sockets to land at her feet.

Then at least there's a happy twist he discovers, since indeed he appears in an afterlife.

In the land of the dead each God remains popular, through but nostalgia, and what matters is how nice you were.

Who was best at being nice? That is the important question in the land of the dead.

Larry waits in the waiting room for someone to explain the tentacles to him.

The waiting room's appearance is exactly the same as the waiting room in the movie *Beetlejuice*.

He wants at least to hear why and how tentacles launched him into space, and why to her and what the fuck.

Then as he waits a glass-cased red rose appears on a seat next to him.

He heads to the counter with the glass case in his hands.

He hands the rose in its glass case to the receptionist, he says, "Someone's red rose and I have no idea..."

The receptionist smiles as if she's seen it before, she says "Larry, let me get your phone number. You... go and live in this land for the dead and take that glass case right along with you. You keep it, and you give it back yourself one day when you can. Don't be an idiot."

"What if no one asks for this, are you kidding me?" Larry worriedly asks.

"Hell, give it to someone else, if you want to. Definitely keep it or give it to someone else. And get out of here. The tentacles happened because they did. Deal with it," the receptionist says.

Then Larry takes the glass case with its red rose and throws it into a trashcan before he sits back down. He hears the glass shatter. He stomps his feet. Then he hears the front door open and there she is. The woman asks him, "Is it true? Where's the rose?" and Larry says "I threw it away," as he gestures with his neck toward the trash.

She walks to the trash as he sits and considers his situation. She pulls from out the trash a shard of glass from the shattered case, he stands, then she stabs him in the left eye with this shard, right in his socket's corner, and an eye of his pops out at her feet again. Then another left eye pops back in his socket, since this is the land of the dead and this is how things work. Then she's more pissed. She wedges the shard into his left eye socket, her hand bleeding while she pushes the shard in. As consequence of her efforts, his face begins to twitch as a new eyeball continuously regenerates in his socket jammed with a shard of glass. But it doesn't hurt because this is the land of the dead. So she stares at him as she walks away and out the room to leave forever, she not realizing the rose thrived without the glass case, there in the trash can, alone.

Larry walks up to the receptionist, the shard in his regenerating eye.

The receptionist shakes her head and laughs and laughs. "You aren't much for advice, honey."

All that's true, and life feeling like a dream damn fine on its own is also true.

Larry sits on his old friend's couch.

"It's been awhile, hasn't it?" his old friend asks.

"Ahh, I had a week of bullshit and who cares," Larry says.

Gus the cat jumps on Larry's lap. His friend the poet asks, "How's the novella coming?" *Ride the Pink Horse* is paused on tv. Larry eases back into the couch. *The Charm of the Highway Strip* plays over the stereo. A car alarm goes off in the street. "I wish someone would steal that car and drive away, or make that car explode to turn off that damn alarm," the poet says. The alarm continues. Gus purrs. Larry's old friend smiles.

www.ingramcontent.com/pod-product-compliance
Lightning Source LLC
Chambersburg PA
CBHW050906180626
46814CB00007B/2913